HERMAN, THE MENTOR

Howard Reede-Pelling

Order this book online at www.trafford.com
or email orders@trafford.com

Most Trafford titles are also available at major online book retailers.

Printed in the United States of America.

ISBN: 978-1-4269-5229-6 (sc)
ISBN: 978-1-4269-5231-9 (e)

Library of Congress Control Number: 2010919284

Trafford rev. 05/03/2011

 www.trafford.com

North America & international
toll-free: 1 888 232 4444 (USA & Canada)
phone: 250 383 6864 ♦ fax: 812 355 4082

CONTENTS

HERMAN, THE MENTOR

IS COVERED BY PENDING COPYRIGHT

This is the tale of a Fishing and Game Inspector who befriends two boys and takes them fishing. He later becomes a family friend and he and his wife and sister become involved with the parents of the boys and a little sister too. They are country folk who run sheep and cattle with a small orchard to help supplement their incomes.

The two boys are prone to getting into tight situations and Herman, the fishing inspector, often has to come to their aid. This is a fast moving story which largely involves the two youngsters and river fishing for trout. It is a good feeling yarn with family type problems and nice outcomes.

CHAPTER ONE

The Fete

Jeremy strained hard upon the ropes of his toboggan. It carried a full cardboard box of apples. It was a very large box; in fact, it was the biggest box he could find in the pile of empties that Mister Jenkins allowed him to select from. Jeremy came to wish that he had not been so ambitious, for in having a very large box; the extra apples added more weight. Now it was his task to drag this heavy load back to the house, as he had faithfully promised his mother he would do. Why Jeremy chose his toboggan as a vehicle instead of his billy-cart, he did not know. Perhaps it may have been the fact that one of the wheels of the billy-cart wobbled dramatically. Jeremy feared that it was about to fall off. Jeremy's father owned a very large farm. There were many sheep, three horses, one of which was the pride and joy of Jeremy, for it was given to him as a birthday present when he became ten years of age. Jeremy really loved his 'Bessie', she was rather old as horses go – the same age as Jeremy in fact – which made her about forty years old in human terms. His father classed her as a 'hack' and ideal in temperament for such an exuberant youngster such as him. On the farm were a couple of windmills, one near the house for personal needs when the tanks were low and the other in the outer paddocks for the hundred head of Herefords that his father cherished, for they were

1

top breeding stock. However sheep were the main source of income and there were eight hundred of them. Three milking cows, a litter of piglets and a run of chickens comprised all of the livestock; not counting the two kelpies his dad needed to round up the stock, of course. Sam and Bluey were really more like family than part of the farm animals though! The orchard covered some three acres and at the time was being harvested. The seasonal pickers were hard at work and when Jeremy was asked by his teacher, Miss Purdie, for something to donate to the school's annual fete; Jeremy suggested that he would ask his parents if they would give some apples. So it happened that the boy was allowed to take as many apples as he could manage, provided that he took only the 'windfalls' – those apples which had fallen to the ground. Jeremy had done so and therefore was struggling and straining to get his huge cardboard box of apples home. He was relieved that his parents had suggested that they would drop the box of apples off at the school, when next they took he and his little sister Karen. The track, over which Jeremy had to drag his toboggan, was in parts grassy but much of it was hard-packed dirt. The boy ceased his struggles for a breather, the while he looked about for some means of assistance. It was at this time that one of the Jersey cows offered her advice.

"Of course!" Jeremy smiled as he mumbled to himself, "Maisy would love to help – I will get some rope!" Jeremy ran to the cow-shed, a happy gleam in his eyes.

The strange sight of one of his milkers being gently led past the kitchen window towards the front verandah, pulling a toboggan upon which was a box full of apples; caused the head of the house-hold to hail his wife.

"Hey Yvonne! Look at young Jeremy, the little scamp!"

"Oh, I always knew our boy was very resourceful!" Yvonne proudly claimed, as she slipped her slim arms about her husband's waist.

"He is a chip off the old block, for sure." Matt nodded as he planted a soft kiss upon his wife's forehead.

"Yes. He is a clever little bloke but I wonder how he is going to lift that heavy box up on to the verandah? Let us slip up to the front door and watch!"

They hurried there and unknown to their son, eagerly witnessed the amazing sight.

Jeremy dragged the wooden lid off the wood box by the back door, lugged it to the small flight of steps where he laid it so he could lead Maisy and enables her to drag his toboggan up the lid and on to the verandah. Leaving the box of apples on the toboggan, the boy led Maisy back to the pasture and released her, with a thankful friendly slap upon the rump. Returning to the verandah, the youngster tugged the toboggan out of the way and up against the wall of the house. His brown eyes sparkled with satisfaction beneath the crop of unruly black hair, which cascaded about the boy's ears. His thin wiry frame straightened as he placed hands upon hips and heaved a heavy sigh of complete satisfaction, for a job well done.

"Gee! I bet Miss Purdie will be very pleased with that lot!" He murmured to himself.

The boy's parents heard the whispered remark and returned to the kitchen to await Jeremy, for they knew he would come to them and explain that the fruit was ready for transportation.

The school fete was a very well patronised event. It was one of the many social happenings that held small country communities together, a chance for hard-working farmers and business people to intermingle and exchange ideas and indeed; help each other with goods and advice. While the adults were conversing or selling the donated goods to assist with the local school's funding, those children not actively participating with the fete, played on the school ground equipment or gathered in isolated corners of the school grounds; discussing those things which were of interest to them.

Jeremy had dutifully spent an hour selling his apples which the cooking class at school had dipped in toffee. He was very happy that they were selling well. His mother urged Jeremy to go and play awhile, as she would look after the stall for him. Grateful to be let off the hook, the youngster eagerly sought his best mate Gerard and the two gleefully ran to the sports oval; to get away from the bustle of the fete. Both were peace-loving souls who could sit and fish for hours with very few words between them. They were quiet, country-bred boys, imbued with common sense and taught to respect nature and enjoy the bounties to be found in the solitude of the bush. As Jeremy and Gerard quietly conversed in the meagre shade afforded by the uprights of the oval fence; they became aware of two teen-agers who strolled across the sports ground and headed towards the timber and brick pavilion. Each had a beer can in one hand and a half-eaten toffee-apple in the other. Cigarettes dangled from their lips.

"That is Joey Gruntz but I do not know the big bloke!" Jeremy whispered to his cobber.

"I think he is a friend of Gruntzy – he is just up for the week-end – I heard my sister talking about him to Flossy Barnes!" Gerard announced.

"Wonder where they are going" Jeremy queried.

"Who cares?" Gerard answered.

"I want to follow them and see, I bet they are up to no good!" Jeremy persisted.

"It is none of our business!" Gerard worried.

The two youngsters stayed where they were as the youths disappeared behind the pavilion. A smashing of glass caused the younger boys to jump up and hurry to see what the cause of the breakage was. Deep down inside they had a good idea what caused it and the bigger boys were heavily suspected. And so it proved. Jeremy and Gerard cautiously peeped in through the broken window, to behold the larrikins causing havoc within the building. They were wilfully tossing any object that was not attached to a solid foundation, from one place to another. The floor was littered with debris. As the younger boys watched, the visitor began to jemmy open lockers with an iron rod, which he had yanked from the window. It was used to bar the window locked. Joey Gruntz suddenly looked to the window and saw the two boys watching.

4

"Get them!" Joey ordered, as he charged towards the boys. By the time the youths were outside the damaged building and had raced around the corner, Jeremy and Gerard were well and truly off the oval and racing back to the fete at the school grounds and the safety of their parents company. The boys raised the alarm which had most of the menfolk and many of the women and children, hurry to the pavilion to witness for themselves, the carnage reported by the two youngsters. Of course the vandals were gone by the time the townsfolk arrived. They were appalled with the wanton destruction. It was apparent that another fund-raiser would now be needed to restore the sporting facility. The stupidity of the destruction caused much chagrin amongst the locals, as council funds were already stretched to the limit. Matt sighed as he noted.

"The pavilion needed restoration but not a complete overhaul, like that which will be necessary now!" Most of those within hearing concurred.

Meanwhile, Joey Gruntz and his city friend were puffing cigarettes as they sprawled atop the wooden garden table by the local picnic barbeque.

"Those little squirts will have dobbed on us by now; we should have grabbed the little blighters when we had the chance!" Joey snarled. His city friend agreed.

"Yeah! And it ain't too late; we got to find them and frighten the living daylights out of them!" Joey shook his head.

"Course it's too late, they've already told; but that don't mean we can't belt the daylights outa them later!"

CHAPTER TWO

The Game Warden

Sunday mornings were quiet times for the farming community. After the cows were milked, the stock fed and the minor chores that fell to the junior members of any family were attended, then it was freedom for those juniors. After the morning church service, of course. Jeremy and Gerard made their way to a favourite fishing area which was easily accessible to the boys. Although they were neighbours, both of their farms were reasonably large and the lads needed to use their bicycles to get to the river from which they fished. As with most waterways, public access was allowed along the banks. Many fishermen, and indeed fisherwomen, could be found restfully whiling away the hours along the winding length of the slow-moving river. The two youngsters found the preferred section where they were wont to fish. It was rather secluded in that the river wound snake-like, leaving a peninsular which was heavily shrubbed amongst the large stand of eucalyptus gums. Their bicycles were easily hidden in the bushes if they chose to do so, but because of the peninsular, there was little need to hide their bicycles at all. If the boys decided to wander the banks, seeking the elusive fish, they could do that without fear of leaving their transport to be stolen. As the two settled down with rods in hand and lines in the water, a chugging splutter sounded as of a motor vehicle in its last stages of demise. The noise was getting closer to the peninsular where Jeremy and Gerard were fishing. Of a sudden, with a final splutter, quiet returned to the bushland as the motor ceased its struggles.

"Must be a fisherman!" Gerard stated.

"Yeah! But the people that fish here usually come from the city and they don't have old rattle-traps!" Jeremy astutely advised. The boys fished in silence.

A murmur of voices alerted the two young fishermen, that they were not alone on their peninsular. Jeremy quickly rose and peered from behind a huge gum down the winding path along which they rode their bicycles earlier. He could see no one. Gerard joined him and together the boys crept from cover to cover towards the voices.

"Crikey!" Jeremy whispered in alarm. "It's that Joey and the new kid – bet they are after us – quick, pack our gear and let's scoot!"

Both boys hurried to their equipment and speedily packed it.

"We should hide our bikes in the bushes and us too!" Gerard panicked.

"No! They could still find us and we'd get killed. Best to make a run for it down the other track!" Jeremy advised.

The boys had their gear strapped to the bicycles and were mounting them, as the two angry young men sighted the terrified boys.

"There they are Lance. Grab the little -!

Too late, the small legs were urging their metal steeds to the utmost and were well out of sight before they could be apprehended.

"Quick – the car – we'll run them down!" Lance shouted.

The bullies raced back to their ancient vehicle, well aware that the children could not out-pace them. The frightened boys groaned as they heard the old vehicle splutter into motion after a couple of mis-firings of the engine.

Four healthy little legs pummelling iron were no match for the ancient machinery of a motor vehicle and the boys were very soon caught up with, by the laughing louts. As the car approached from the rear, Jeremy cast a terrified glance behind, to behold the car almost upon him. He veered heavily to his left to let it pass but in doing so, collided with his friend. Both screaming boys crashed into a large shrub, where they lay tangled together with their bicycles on top of them and legs entwined in the machines. Their fall was cushioned by the bush and they were not seriously injured. The car skidded to a stop and two happy louts approached the stricken youngsters.

"Gotcha, you pair of snivelling little blabber-mouths!"

Joey snarled as he lifted the bikes to get at the children.

"This one's mine!"

Lance called as he dragged the fair-haired Gerard out of the bushes and threw him to the middle of the track, where he delivered a hefty kick to the little boy's ribs. Gerard screamed in agony as Jeremy received like treatment from Joey.

"Let's toss them into the river!" Lance urged.

"Hey, what a great idea!" Joey agreed. "Come on you two; time for a swim!"

Each youth yanked a boy to his feet and shoved the unwilling and very sore little boys ahead of them, to the river; which parallelled the bush track. The youths were in the act of swinging the two youngsters off their feet and into the river, when a loud stentorian voice hailed.

"Oy! What is going on there?"

The voice belonged to a very large fisherman who happened to be passing and noted the car and fallen bicycles. His keen, alert eyes bristling with anger beneath a floppy fishing hat bedecked with flies and lures, as he hurried to the suspicious scene.

"Whatcha want?" The belligerent city lout ordered.

The man saw the terrified looks upon the faces of the two little boys turn to relief, as they attempted to go to the newcomer.

"They want to toss us into the river!" Gerard snivelled.

"No we weren't!" Joey defended.

"We just brought them here to wash up, 'cause they fell off their bikes!"

"You tried to run us down!" Jeremy accused.

"Did not – you panicked as we were trying to pass!"

Joey hissed his grip on the boy's arm tightened fiercely.

"Ouch! You are hurting me!" Jeremy cried.

"Let the boys go or I will break your rotten necks!"

The fisherman charged forwards, fists ready to thrash these bullies.

"Come on, let's go. These little brats are ungrateful liars anyway!"

Lance and Joey beat a hasty retreat to their dilapidated vehicle. Before driving off, each drove a hefty foot into the spokes of a bicycle. They drove away, still threatening dire reprisals upon the two boys who seemed to thwart them each time they met.

"Thank you Mister!" Jeremy reached out to shake the man by the hand. He responded and asked.

"Do you boys know these bullies?"

"Only Joey Gruntz, the little one. We don't know who the big one is except that he comes from the city!" Jeremy softly said, still trembling with fright.

"They wrecked our sports pavilion and we saw them, that's why they kicked us!" Gerard spoke up, and then began to sniffle as he added. "They were going to drown us!"

He broke down completely.

"There, there!" The big man patted the tiny shoulders. "Don't cry little man, it is all over now. Let us see if your bicycles are damaged!"

He led the way and asked what they meant by saying that the youths kicked them.

"When they dragged the bikes off and threw us onto the road – they kicked us – look, see the sore part?" Jeremy raised his shirt and singlet, exposing his ribs.

"Wow! That is a nasty bruise – what about you son?"

The man kneeled down as Gerard exposed his ribs too.

"The rotten hounds, I wish that I knew about this before – no – perhaps it is better that I did not know. You poor little blokes! Here are your bicycles – gosh - you certainly wrecked them; didn't you?"

Both machines had a buckled wheel.

"Gee! We did not hit anything, we just fell off into the bushes; how did they get bent like that?" The man noted the youth-sized footprints but said nothing to the children.

"Listen boys – er – what are your names?" The man asked. They told him.

"I am Herman Gordon. Now I know your parents have warned you not to ride with strangers, but your cycles are broken and you are much bruised. I really think I should drive you and your bicycles home!"

"It is all right thank you Mister Gordon. We live on these two farms. That big blue gum is the border of Gerard's place to the right and my dad owns the one to the left. It goes all the way to the hills over there!" Jeremy pointed to the hills in question.

"But your homes must be kilometres apart and kilometres away, I can't even see a house from here. It is too far for you to walk, especially with those bruises!" Herman worried.

"We will get into worse trouble if we get into a stranger's car – I know dad will kill me – or worse!" Jeremy frowned.

"Do you know what this is?" Herman asked of the boys as he produced an official badge.

"Wow!" Gerard gasped. "It is a Game Warden's Badge and it has your name on it – Herman Gordon!"

"Yes. I am a Game Warden and I am on duty to catch people taking under-sized fish at the moment. Now, if I give each of you a piece of note book and a pen, will you write down my name, car registration number and what type and colour vehicle it is; put the papers in your pockets and then I can drive you home to your parents – is that okay!"

Jeremy looked at Gerard, who nodded.

"Yes, I suppose that would be all right!" Jeremy said. He looked at Herman, and then asked.

"Do you have a car 'phone?" Herman gasped.

"Well, blow me down – of course – how stupid of me!"

A telephone call to both boys' parents dispelled all doubts and the bicycles were placed in the back of the four-wheel-drive. Herman and the boys enjoyed a leisurely drive to their homes, where he was welcomed with cups of tea and thanked profusely for his timely intervention. The local police station was notified of the larrikin behaviour of the teenagers and they were heavily fined and made to do community work. Lance had to return to the city, his fine and community work was to be attended there. Until his sentence was duly satisfied, the teenager was not to return. It was a stipulation by the magistrate, that both youths should be separated until the court orders were no longer valid. A major part of those court orders was that the two young boys were to be left alone and no contact with them by the youths would be tolerated.

CHAPTER THREE

Herman's Secret Spot

Having had this explained to them, both Jeremy and Gerard felt safe to return to their fishing peninsular. The first stipulation of the magistrate was that the damaged bicycles should be repaired by the fines imposed upon the youths. With restored bicycles, once more the young boys pedalled to their destination.

"Do you know how Joey and that Lance bully found us that day Jeremy?"

Gerard asked, his eyes alight with hidden knowledge.

"No. I wondered about that!" Jeremy turned wide brown eyes to his cobber. "How did they know where we were?"

"Dad told me that Flossie Barnes let them know where we were fishing, because they asked her if she knew and because we always fish at the same place; it was easy. They just followed the path and they knew we rode our bikes because they followed the wheel marks; that is what dad said!" Gerard informed, and then added. "My dad reckons if he meets those two bullies he is going to belt the daylights out of them!"

"Yair. So is mine. But mum says he is not to, because they have already been punished by the police!" Jeremy rubbed where his bruise was almost healed; then whinged. "That is all right for them, they did not have to suffer sore ribs like we did."

"That's right!" Gerard agreed.

As the boys began the ride along the path where they usually fished, Gerard queried.

"Hey, Jeremy! What say we go somewhere else to fish – we always fish the peninsular. We may have better luck at a new spot?"

"Okay!" Jeremy enthused. "And I know just the spot too. I can remember dad taking me fishing about two kilometres upstream from here, there is a real grouse spot where the river narrows a bit and it flows a lot faster. Lots of little backwaters and eddies; we are sure to get trout or big redfin there - let's go!"

The youngsters happily pedalled their way along the river track.

After about half an hour of fishing, both lads had caught something worthwhile. Gerard had two one kilo redfin and Jeremy had the prize of the day; a one and a half kilo brown trout. It seemed huge to the boys, for although more often than not they did catch a fish, of late the fish had been small or just of size; mostly they were redfin. This trout was the catch of a life-time.

"Told you it would be good to change spots for once!" Gerard boasted, as he jealously eyed the nice trout.

Jeremy placed the fish between fern fronds and put it in his creel. A stranger with very expensive fishing tackle came into view from upstream.

"How is the fishing boys?" He asked.

"Very good Mister!" Jeremy showed off their catch.

"What wonderful fish!" The stranger exclaimed. "Do you mind if I join you and fish here too?"

"No Mister, but we were just leaving – we have to go!" Gerard advised as he began packing his fishing tackle. Jeremy followed suit. As they were leaving, another fisherman entered the scene. It was Herman Gordon, the Game Warden.

"Hello boys!" He greeted them. "Gerard, isn't it – and Jeremy?" Herman nodded to the other fisherman. "How is the fishing?" He asked.

"No good. I just arrived here, been fishing upstream for an hour, then came here – have not caught anything yet – the boys did though. Little blokes make a man look foolish with all my expensive equipment!" Herman nodded.

"It is always the way though, isn't it?" He turned his attention to the youngsters, who politely stood by. "Suppose I had better do my job and check your catch – eh boys?" He smiled genially.

"Gosh Mister Gordon, will we get fined?"

"No Jeremy, we always have to make allowances for children, because they do not always know the law regarding fishing. If your fish are under-sized, we let you off with a warning. Let me see what you have – I am sure they are really whoppers!"

"Take my word for it, they are!" The other fisherman noted, albeit a little miffed.

"Wow! No doubt about that, eh boys?" Herman gasped as he saw the youngster's catches.

"You must be very experienced fishermen. Those beauties are well over the limit. Well done lads!"

Both boys displayed huge grins upon their faces. Herman chatted for a few minutes to the stranger.

"Goodbye Mister Gordon!"

Jeremy called, as he and Gerard wheeled their bicycles over to the track. Herman waved; then offered.

"Oh boys! Are you going to fish elsewhere?"

"No Sir, we are off home now, we do not want the fish to spoil!"

"Hang on; I was going to call on your folks as I left your 'phone numbers at home. Would you come to my car please, I left the 'phone there?"

"Yes Mister Gordon, but why do you have to go to my house. Have we done something wrong?"

Herman seemed to forever have a smile on his face. He was a jovial sort of chap and there was a merry twinkle in his eyes as he walked with the two children along the path upstream, to where he left his four wheel drive vehicle.

"Not at all boys, no, I wanted to take you to a very private part of the river where I fish. It is one of the most secluded fishing spots on the river – my own special place – and you can not get bothered by anyone whilst fishing there."

"Gosh, how come?" Gerard asked in awe.

"Two reasons." Herman informed. "Firstly, it is off the beaten track and so hidden that no one knows about it. The second reason is that it is too dangerous a place for you boys to be in alone; so I will always be with you when you fish there!"

Jeremy looked at Gerard with wide open eyes.

"Gee! I don't think my dad will let us!" He worried.

"That is why I wanted to contact your folks – to ask them. Of course, maybe you boys may not want to fish with me, perhaps you would rather fish alone?"

The boys again exchanged looks, both nodded.

"Gee, it is very nice of you Mister Gordon, but why do you want to take us to your special fishing spot. Do we have to do something?" Jeremy asked, a little shamefully. "I mean – like get your bait or something like that?"

Herman laughed.

"No, I always get my own bait or I bring fresh bait with me on my fishing trips. You will have to get your own bait too - but I can help you there!"

"Is there a reason why you want to take us then?" Jeremy persisted, a worried frown upon his little face.

"Yes Jeremy, there is a reason!"

Both youngsters looked expectantly to the Game Warden. He elaborated.

"I was disgusted that two little boys could not fish in safety from MY River. I need for you to be safe and to feel safe after your nasty fright. Also, because you are very polite and well-mannered, I know you can keep my special spot secret – we do not want everybody to try and fish there – there are plenty of other parts of the river to fish!"

Gerard said for both of them.

"Gosh Mister Gordon, we would love that and it is very good of you, but I don't know if our parents will let us. Can you ask them please and when can we go there?"

"First I want you to put your catch in my ice-box to keep the fish from going off; it is in the back seat area, on the floor!"

When the boys obeyed, Herman reached for his telephone. As the day was still young and Herman was known and respected by the children's parents, permission was granted. Both families expressed satisfaction with the arrangement; for they felt their off-spring would be quite safe and well looked after, by an official. They could rest easy for their children's safety.

It was a rough drive of about three kilometres to Herman Gordon's secret fishing area. The almost nothing of a track veered off to the left of the gravel road, which abounded the rear of the property owned by Jeremy's father. The track initially was a well-used path to the river, then after about two hundred metres of travel parallel to it; the river itself veered off to the left. Herman's secret spot was another finger of land just like the peninsular where the boys usually fished. The difference being that this particular peninsular was very heavily shrubbed and huge trees rose ever higher into the sky. The area was virgin wilderness and it was fenced off with cyclone wire fencing. A gate gave access and Gerard had the honour of unlocking and re-locking the gate, after the vehicle had entered.

"Gosh Mister Gordon, why is it fenced off?" Jeremy asked in awe.

Gerard climbed into the cabin of the vehicle as Herman answered the boy's query.

"This is council property and I am in charge. There is a hut and storage shed further into the bushes, with a lean-to as a garage for my four wheel drive. This is my headquarters from which I travel the river to keep law and order. It is really a council depot!"

"Wow!" Gerard gasped. "Your own private fishing spot! Can anyone walk the banks fishing here?"

"No – not at all. This is one area exclusively for council workers. There are signs erected at each end of the fence where the river enters and leaves; warning people not to trespass on the fenced off land –

for security reasons – you see, the shed holds explosives so it has to be very secure. Anyway, there are no paths along the riverbank in this peninsular. The scrub is very thick and almost impassable. I would appreciate it if you two do not tell anyone about this depot – only your parents – but please ask them not to mention it! Can I count on you?"

He eyed them seriously.

"Yes Mister Gordon!" They chorused.

Two very eager and excited little boys followed Herman along an almost imperceptible track through very dense undergrowth. They were warned to be watchful for snakes as the peninsular was thick with them. Each child was issued with a freshly cut curved staff taken from a weeping willow tree. They were taught the proper and correct way to use them – only if it were necessary – otherwise leave the creatures alone. The snakes were entitled to be there as it was their home after all.

Herman stood by a rotted log until the boys were close beside him. Warning them to be watchful for snakes, he rolled the log over and they fossicked for worms, grubs and little frogs. Herman rummaged through his fishing bag and extracted three containers with air holes punctured through the lids. One for the two frogs they caught, one for the variety of grubs from the ground and out of the rotted wood and the third, heaped with tiger-worms and one long scrub-worm. He sprinkled a little damp soil in with the bait. The best fishing area was from behind a huge willow. It had a snag free inlet at either side of it and the tree was good cover so that any trout which happened by, may not notice the eager fishermen lurking. Further along was a rather large, open grassy-banked beach. Both boys immediately grasped its best use.

"Gee Mister Gordon, what a ripper spot to go swimming. Can we have a swim?"

It was Jeremy, the bold one, who made this suggestion.

"No! We are fishing today and the water is to remain quiet. Anyway, we do not have swimming costumes."

"Arrgh!" Jeremy moaned. "We can go without – we don't need costumes!"

Herman gave the boys a most severe look.

"Not in my river you don't. One day when you have your costumes and your parents blessing, maybe then I will let you swim here!"

CHAPTER FOUR

A Smelly Little Man

The figure of a weedy little man lurking about the verandah of Jenkins General Store was noticeable purely because of the furtive glances cast hither and yon. He was a middle-aged ruffian of some thirty-nine years and scraggy unkempt hair bothered his vision. A long, lank moustache dribbled down either side of his chin and dark glasses hid his sneaky eyes. It appeared that the man slept in his rather dishevelled clothing and the much used sneakers upon his feet, needed to be cast aside. It was obvious that he was 'casing' the premises, no doubt, with robbery in mind. When the last customer left with her bag of goodies, Terrence Grail casually sauntered in; having first cast quick glances about to be sure no other customers were coming. Hiram Jenkins welcomed all customers with a happy smile, no matter what their position on the social scale.

"Howdy! What can I do for you?" The proprietor asked.

Terrence pointed a sharpened screwdriver at the hapless store owner; then demanded.

"Empty the till – now!"

Without a word, it was done. Terrence Grail hurriedly quit the premises with the cash stuffed down his shirt front, and with not even a backwards glance, shuffled away. Hiram immediately rang the local Police Station.

. . . .

The three fishermen caught a mixed bag. Herman caught three one kilo trout, while Jeremy caught one and a redfin. The redfin was a little small and when Herman pouted at its size and tilted his head, Jeremy dutifully released it back into the water; the fish flipped, and then swam away. Gerard caught one more redfin and it was much larger than the two he caught earlier. The boy was quite elated with his days fishing.

"Time to go home lads!" Herman stated.

"Gee! Can we come again one day, Mister Gordon, please!" Jeremy politely asked.

Gerard expectantly awaited the answer.

"Well you did behave well and were obedient. Perhaps next week – we will ask your parents when I take you home!"

"Yay!" Two exuberant youngsters shouted in unison.

Both boys were praised for the good catches, by their respective parents. The parents were quite happy to allow the boys to go fishing with Herman Gordon; when ever he felt he could manage them. If it was not too much trouble and he was sure that the lads did behave properly and were not a burden to him. Assuring the families that he actually enjoyed their company, as he and his wife were as yet childless; he deemed it good preparation against the time that they had their own little ones running about. Herman went home to his wife very happy at having been of service to the people who contributed to his wages, and with boxes of goodies from both farms; a box of fresh apples from Jeremy's folks and a fresh picking of black grapes from Gerard's vineyard.

As Herman drove home, he noticed a stranger walking the same road as he was travelling. He offered the man a lift, which was accepted. The man was an unsavoury looking character and the Game Warden noticed a peculiar odour about the rough-appearing man.

"Going far?" Herman asked.

"No, just to the river; can you drop me off near the river?"

20

Herman nodded.

"Sure, camping there are you?"

"N – Yes, yes I am camping there – just overnight!"

His words did not ring true; still, it was none of Herman's business unless the man wilfully damaged property, lit fires or kept under-sized or illegal fish. Herman was glad when the smelly little man left the vehicle to wander off along a track which Herman knew, led to a small area often frequented by fisher-folk. 'Strange bloke' he thought to himself. 'Wonder what he is up to? Hasn't got a car or he would not have been walking, so if he is camping, he must be a tramp – certainly looked like it – I won't miss not seeing him any more!' When Herman arrived home and emptied his vehicle of fishing tackle and other odds and sods – such as his car 'fridge – he found a five dollar note on the floor of his four wheel drive.

"Crikey!" He ejaculated. "Must have dropped it, that vagabond, I will call on him in the morning, he may still be about."

Meanwhile, unknown to Herman, the little man who robbed the General Store, had turned the township into a beehive of activity and much discussion. Police were taking statements of the locals in the near vicinity and were having leaflets with the robber's identikit and other known details; made up for distribution around the district.

Jenkins General Store had a reward poster on the window, offering fifty dollars for information leading to the capture of the ruffian. Hiram Jenkins had his own description of the robber written on the reward poster. News travels very quickly about small communities. Herman Gordon put two and two together and came up with a winner. Yes, the chap he gave a ride to must certainly be the robber and the money found, was no doubt part of the stolen cash. He notified the local police of his suspicions and arranged to meet one of the local detectives near the drop-off point. Both officials made their way to the camp site which Herman knew the suspect would have deserted by now. A camp site with warm ashes was located; however there was nobody other than themselves in the area. They knew a search of the locality would prove fruitless, so consequently, they returned to their usual occupations. Herman was reminded to keep watch for the suspect during his rounds. The detective returned to his station to explore other avenues for the detention of the man who so blatantly robbed the local store.

Jeremy arrived home from school the next day. It was the Monday and both he and Gerard had boasted often to their school friends, of their wonderful fishing experiences, their good catches and the fact of a special fishing place that was to be kept secret – they had promised. Much pleading and cajoling could not make them reveal their great secret. Both boys were revered by their following. Jeremy began his after school chores, such as feeding and watering the domestic stock, sweeping the verandas and tidying up the wood shed, etcetera. Those things done, he went to the horse yard to talk to his hack, Bessie. She was happy to see him and welcomed his light touch on her nose, she nuzzled against his chest.

"Pleased to see me Bessie, are you? I bet you want me to take you for a run – hang on – I will ask mum!"

Jeremy eagerly saddled up after his mother consented on the proviso that he would only be away for a half hour, and with a firm promise that he would not leave the property.

"Yes Mum – I promise!" He agreed and raced to get the most out of his half hour.

Bessie was frisky and needed a run, so Jeremy set off at a brisk trot. Their direction was to the North paddock where most of his father's stock was grazing. He could gallop freely there, providing he kept clear of the sheep, so as not to alarm them. A stampede would run their condition down, and be detrimental to their market value. Dutifully, Jeremy closed the home paddock gate. In doing so, he noticed bicycle tracks and they were identical to his own bicycles treads. The boy knew he had not been that way on his bicycle recently. Usually he rode through the East paddock gate on his way to Gerard's farm; then the two would ride South to the river. What was his bicycle tracks doing at the North gate? Jeremy decided to follow the tracks. Perhaps they were not from his bicycle at all. Maybe it was some visitor, they would have returned, surely; leaving two sets of tracks. But then, there was only one set of tracks. Apprehensively, Jeremy galloped Bessie in the direction the bicycle would have taken, to the next gate. Sure enough, the tracks continued and the boy followed. After travelling for a kilometre, Jeremy noticed up ahead, a minute figure. It appeared to be a cyclist! Jeremy urged Bessie to greater speed and before long they were almost upon the hurrying cyclist. The rider heard the galloping horse and cast furtive, terrified looks behind, the while he pedalled his energy to a standstill. Jeremy looked down at his bicycle with anger on his face and hurt in his heart.

"Hey! That is my bicycle you thief; give it back!"

Terrence Grail alighted from the vehicle, breathless, a frightened look on his face; then he beheld the youthful pursuer. His bravado returned.

"So what! What are you going to do about it?"

Terrence snarled as he attempted to mount the bicycle again.

"Get him Bessie!" Jeremy urged his steed forwards against the cyclist.

Bessie nudged the machine over, toppling Terrence to the ground; she whinnied in anger. Terrified of being trampled, the man hastened away on foot; leaving the bicycle to its owner. When the thief was a safe distance away and was still going, Jeremy dismounted and checked his bicycle for damage. It was unbroken.

The sight of Jeremy returning home astride his bicycle and leading Bessie left his parents awaiting him on the back verandah in amazement and demanding an explanation. That done, the police were notified of the latest sighting of the little vagrant, who was suspected of the daylight robbery of Jenkins Store.

CHAPTER FIVE

A Fright – Then Bliss

Peace and quiet returned to the township. Although the vagrant was not apprehended, and school days were tranquil as usual; two young ten-year-olds were eagerly awaiting the coming week-end in the hope of returning to Herman's secret fishing spot. Each time the telephone rang on Friday evening, Jeremy expected it was Mister Gordon to invite them swimming or fishing. Jeremy hoped it would be both. They could fish first while the bush was still, then after that it would not matter if the area echoed to the shrill voices of children romping. Saturday morning came and still no response from Herman Gordon. Jeremy asked if he could telephone Gerard to see if he had heard anything. Jeremy's mother smiled a little sadly as she reflected.

"You know Dear, Mister Gordon did not say for sure that he would be taking you fishing. He may have other things to do this week-end. If you ring Gerard, Mister Gordon will not be able to ring us because the line will be busy. I am sure he will ring sometime but don't expect to go with him every week-end!"

Both boys fretted as they did the chores expected of them. Jeremy was returning the empty buckets to the milking shed, when his mother called to him from the verandah.

"Jeremy, there is a call for you!"

Eagerly the boy raced inside, his heart beating excitedly. The call was from Gerard, he had received a call from Herman Gordon. They were not going fishing with him that day as he had to work. Jeremy exhaled a disappointed gasp.

"Ah gee! What rotten luck – I wanted to go fishing!"

Gerard could hold his news no longer and blurted.

"But he did say if we go to church on Sunday morning, he will take us fishing in the afternoon, and – and – then we can swim if we bring our swimmers and a towel!"

"Yippee!" Came from Jeremy, then excitedly. "Did your mum say you can go?"

Gerard nodded, even though his playmate could not see him.

"Yep! But only if you can come too – hurry – ask your mum, go on, quick!"

A hurried verbal exchange between Jeremy and his mother had all arrangements for the Sunday finalised; which left both boys with a free Saturday until the evening chores were due. The children were not allowed to go fishing that day. Their parents deemed one exciting day would be enough for them. The boys would have to do something else. They arranged to go riding on their horses.

Two young equestrians were walking their mounts along the boundary fence of Jeremy's father's property. The boys were expected to stay inside the boundaries of their properties. When they came to the huge blue gum which was the marker for the boundary both properties', it was necessary to exit one gate onto council owned land where the gravel road was, and then enter the gate of Gerard's father's property. Jeremy was leaning over from his mount to secure his gate (each child's duty was to secure his own gate) and Gerard was about to open the gate to his father's property; when Rosie reared in fear of a snake stretched out in the shade of the gate. With a terrified scream Rosie bolted along the gravel road. Taken by surprise, Gerard hung on grimly the while he struggled to control his excited hack. Jeremy galloped in pursuit. Rosie bolted for almost a kilometre before Gerard was able to pacify the mare and bring her to a halt. Jeremy had overtaken them and eased Bessie across the front of

Rosie, making her veer off into the scrub lining the river. Both lads dismounted and tied their mares to strong scrub trees. They needed to let Rosie and Bessie settle down by allowing them to graze on the lush grasses along the waterway. The two boys sauntered to the river bank which was only a matter of forty metres away. They sat on the grassy river bank and threw sticks into the water, to watch them float away as they conversed. All was quiet and peaceful, when a sharp crack as of a dry stick snapping underfoot, alerted the boys to the fact that they were not alone. When they turned their heads in the direction of the disturbance, Terrence Grail was almost upon them. The two boys stayed seated, fearfully eying the man they both knew was a dangerous robber and thief. Although only a small man, the boys too, were small and he appeared to tower over them.

"So!" He gloated. "You curly-haired little crumb – you tried to trample me with your horse, didn't you. Where are your bikes; I am going to toss them into the river!"

"Bessie did not try to trample you; she was just pushing you off my bicycle that you stole!" Jeremy defended.

"Stole nothing!" Terrence snarled. "I was just borrowing it; I would have put it back!"

"I don't believe you. Once a thief always a thief!" Jeremy mumbled.

Terrence slapped the boy across his curly black locks, shouting.

"Shut up before I give you both a thrashing – where are your bikes – you have hidden them, haven't you?"

As Jeremy held his sore head, Gerard jumped up and kicked Terrence in the shins. When the man grabbed at his grazed leg, Jeremy gave him a great shove. Terrence fell to the ground shouting blue murder. Both boys nimbly raced to their trusty hacks and galloped off to their respective homes. Jeremy was the first to arrive home and alert his folks to the whereabouts of the dangerous man in the neighbourhood. It was the second time that the boy had come into contact with the wanted fugitive, so a desperate father demanded an immediate search for the man; by the authorities. A hurried posse of townsfolk, including the boy's fathers, were enlisted to aid the local police to apprehend the villain.

The search along the river bank proved fruitful and Terrence Grail was taken into custody and charged; not only with the robbery of the store, but also with one count of theft of a bicycle and intimidating a minor with physical force. Most of the stolen money was recovered as the robber had been unable to spend it anywhere; through lack of transport. Jeremy was taken by his very proud parents to Jenkins General Store, where he was given the promised fifty dollars reward money announced for the arrest of the robber. Jeremy immediately donated it to the funds for the restoration of the sports pavilion. Mister Jenkins was so moved by the boy's generous gesture, that he gave a further five dollars to both Jeremy and Gerard – just for their own personal spending. The fathers of both boys matched it.

That night Jeremy's parents popped in to tuck him in to bed.

"We are very proud of you Son, especially for the way you donated the reward money back to the community.

"That was very generous of you; what made you think of that Son?" His father asked.

Jeremy reddened as he accepted the praise, and then answered.

"Well, I use the sports pavilion too and the sooner the money is gathered, the sooner we can use it!"

"Sleep tight Jeremy Dear, and have pleasant dreams. You have a big day tomorrow with Mister Gordon, remember?" His mother gave him a peck on the forehead. "Goodnight!"

"Night Ma – 'night Pa!"

Both boys' parents had seen to it that there were ample drinks and sandwiches prepared, for the fishing and swimming excursion. The boys were reminded to do as Mister Gordon asked of them.

"And do not forget to behave properly!"

Jeremy's father called, as the boy waved from Herman's four wheel drive; when they were leaving to go and collect Gerard. Herman too, had come well prepared. Fresh sausages, rissoles, tomatoes and onions, along with fruit and drinks; was his contribution. They were going to have a barbeque lunch!

"Wow!" Exclaimed Gerard. "We have enough food to sink a ship; what will we do with it all?"

"We can feed our sandwiches to the birds – I would rather have sausages!"

Jeremy eagerly answered. Herman firmly squashed that line of thought.

"No boys that is not a good idea. Firstly because it is a waste of food, secondly, you must not feed wild birds and animals as it is detrimental to their well-being; and thirdly, the most important thing is – someone may be in need of it – perhaps ourselves. In the bush, you both should know you must keep emergency rations. What if you go wandering and get lost – have to stay out overnight – you would welcome it then!"

As it was noon when Herman came to pick up his young fishing companions, the three arrived within half an hour at their destination and immediately got their fishing tackle out to enjoy the fishing; while the area was quiet and peaceful. Herman knew that the cooking time, boys will be boys and the scrub may echo to much laughter and merriment. So they fished in the peace and serenity of the native bush, enjoying the solitude, the bush smells and those noises such as the carolling of birdlife and the scratching of Koalas and other native animals; which were often to be witnessed going about their daily life.

Herman caught his usual couple of trout, on occasions it was three, if one of the first two was a little small – just of size – then he would fish for a third. Jeremy was a most disappointed youngster as he had no luck at all, but Gerard was successful with one very nice brown trout. Down in the mouth somewhat, Jeremy claimed hunger was assailing him.

"Mister Gordon" he asked "May I go and get a sandwich please?"

"No Jeremy! I can not let you wander about here alone, it is too dangerous. I think we should all pack up and go for our barbeque!"

"Can't I stay here until it is ready – the trout are biting?"

Gerard frowned as he asked. Herman shook his head.

"Sorry, it is just as dangerous to leave you here alone – I will not hear if you slip into the river – come on Lad, pack up; we can come back after lunch. Remember, you cannot go swimming straight after lunch, so we can fish then for an hour or so!"

"Oh yeah! Let's have lunch!" Gerard packed up quickly.

The lunchtime barbeque was a great experience for the two exuberant youngsters. Sure, they had attended barbeques before, both at home, at a friend's places and at the school fetes. Nothing could compare with this one in a small grassed clearing amid virgin bushland not far from a trout-filled river and where they were allowed to cook for themselves, guided by an experienced bush cook; such as their hero – Mister Gordon!

Three very replete fishermen lazed under the gums and willows which lined the idyllic river scene. All had indulged too well in the eye-catching scrumptious barbeque meal of fried sausages, rissoles, tomatoes and onions, sprinkled with a light dusting of basil. The campsite cleaned up and the goodies and utensils repacked; all three returned to do some more fishing. Whilst the boys idly and silently watched their lines, Herman dozed as he leaned against a willow tree. For him, it was siesta time. An hour passed.

"Mister Gordon, wake up, it is getting hot and it is time to go swimming!"

Jeremy shook his guardian's shoulder.

"Eh? What's that?" Herman roused. Gerard enlightened him.

"May we go for a swim now, please?" Herman pulled both hands down over his waking eyes.

"Goodness, I must have dozed off. What time is it boys?"

"Two o'clock – fourteen hundred!" Jeremy said.

"Catch anything?" The man asked. Gerard replied.

"Only a redfin each and a little one I had to release – you snored!"

"Ha -ha, did I? Sorry lads. Come on then, let us go to the truck and pack our gear away; then we will get into our swimmers!"

"Yay!" All hurried to the base.

CHAPTER SIX

The Outing

Herman's hut was a two roomed one. It comprised of a small kitchen with three-seat benches either side of a table which abutted a wall just below the window. The other room had two bunks in it and there was no room for anything else. Herman allowed the boys to use the hut first to change, while he went to the storage shed and gathered a light nylon rope and a tomahawk. He had the boys wait outside while he donned his own swimming gear. There was already a stout tree at the downstream end of the small sandy beach. Herman placed the tomahawk at the base of the tree and tied one end of the rope to the tree, the rest of the rope he left coiled upon the ground.

"What are they for Mister Gordon?" Jeremy asked a puzzled expression on his face.

"Just a safeguard Son if one of you gets into difficulty I can throw the rope in before I rescue you, then it is easy to get ashore!"

"And the tomahawk?" Gerard asked.

"In case I need to cut a sapling down to fight the crocodiles!" He grinned.

"Crocodiles?" Both boys gasped.

"There are no crocodiles in here are there?" Gerard's wide light blue eyes were alight with alarm as he asked.

"No! I was just kidding – it is safe to swim here – the tomahawk is to make a path through the bushes later. I want to get to another fishing spot just upstream a little, and I will have to hack a way through the heavy scrub!"

For almost an hour the boys splashed and swam about. They thoroughly enjoyed themselves, especially in the last fifteen minutes when they enticed Herman to join them. He hoisted the two in turn to his shoulders where they dived into the deeper parts of the water; after Herman had checked for snags or driftwood. The three sunned themselves as they stretched out to dry in the warm afternoon sun. Herman donned his heavy boots after the trio had dressed and he led the boys to the beach again. He re-coiled the rope which he slung over his shoulder, then taking the tomahawk, began to cut a way through the dense undergrowth. Jeremy and Gerard followed at a sensible distance. Much of the shrubbery was just that – shrubbery – bushes growing thickly together. It was not at all that difficult to force a path through the majority of it. Only occasionally was Herman in need of using the small axe, it was mainly creepers and ivy barring the way. He began to think that a machete would have been a more suitable tool than the tomahawk. Eventually they came to the area that Herman was seeking. It was actually a quite large backwater and it was very deep.

"A real fishing hole!" Herman stated. "Tuft grasses on the edge of grassy banks, is ideal trout water!"

"Wow!" Gasped both boys.

"What a ripper spot. Maybe there is the grand-daddy of all trout hiding in that deep hole; can we go and get our rods please Mister Gordon – please – pretty please?" Jeremy begged.

Herman began to shake his head but caught sight of the very disappointed and hurt expression upon Gerard's face.

"Oh, I suppose a half hour can be spared, but then we must leave immediately I ask; will you promise that – no snivelling – we just pack up and leave?"

"Yes Sir!"

All made their way quietly back to get the fishing gear again. The trio found it most difficult to force their way through the dense

31

shrubbery. Fishing rods and creels are not the easiest things to manage, with bushes and twigs getting tangled in the lines and the drag of those creels became irksome. A half an hour of quiet fishing produced good catches all round. Herman caught the first trout and it was a whopper of two kilos. He called it a day for himself, as he had all the fish he needed for just him and his wife. Herman explained to his wards that one never wastes; it is better to leave good fishing for others and not be greedy just to waste fish. Both boys caught two trout each and with their other fish already on ice, they were happy to leave when requested to do so, by Herman.

"Won't your parents be proud of you boys when you get home with your very nice catches?" He asked.

"My word Mister Gordon. I know my dad will be happy for me - - mum might not be though – she hates scaling fish!" Gerard enlightened him.

"Well, one day I will show you the bushman's way to cook fresh fish and the way that is done; you do not have to scale them. What about you Jeremy, does your mum like cooking fish?"

Jeremy off-handedly drawled.

"Ah no, Mum does not mind but Dad usually cooks them on our outdoor barbeque. We have a one-fire stove with a hot plate on top and Dad usually rolls the fish in tin-foil with lots of butter and they come out beautiful – the skin just peels off when it is cooked!"

"Sounds very much like my bush cook way, only I use very damp newspapers and roll the fish in them in the embers. It does the same job but when you peel away the newspaper, the scales come off with it!"

Jeremy and Gerard were extremely tired after their very big day, especially so considering the excitement of the preceding day. They sat in Herman's four wheel drive, almost asleep. Herman let them rest while he drove them home. Gerard was to be the first home and he awoke as the vehicle rattled over their cattle-grid.

"Gosh. We are nearly home!" He ejaculated. Jeremy came alive too.

"I think I dozed off!" He murmured.

"Yes, you both had a bit of a snooze, but you have to come alive now lads. Do not forget to pack your gear away as soon as you get in and refrigerate the fish. Then you must do your chores – so no more snoozing – wakey – wakey!"

Both boys thanked Herman for the wonderful outing he had provided for them and of course, asked when next they could go fishing and swimming. It was a little bit of a damper when the big man told them he was not sure; he would have to contact their parents to arrange something. It most certainly would not be the following week-end though. Herman had other plans arranged. When they were dropped off at their respective homes, each boy did not have to be reminded to thank Herman for the lovely fishing trip. Each lad pre-empted his parent's thoughts and loudly thanked Herman again. He drove home somewhat melancholy as these youngsters were beginning to get to him and he began to long for a family of his own. 'I must have a word to Moira about this, perhaps if I soften her up by arranging to have her come on the next fishing excursion when I take the boys!' He mused. He thought back over the day's events and the happy smiling faces of two wonderfully polite, happy little lads. His eyes softened and he wondered at the joy and good feelings he had; of a job well done!

Two weeks had passed and everyday life went on as usual. Herman did not ring to arrange a fishing outing with the boys and they began to think that maybe Mister Gordon had forgotten about them. Gerard was moved to comment during one of the school breaks.

"He is probably too busy or he does not like us anymore. Gee, we were having fun and his fishing spot is much better than ours – we will probably never hear from him again!"

Jeremy was more optimistic.

"Rats! Mister Gordon is just too busy. Most of his work days are at the week-ends; that is when all the city fishermen hang around - he has to work then. That is what inspectors are for – they have to stop people from taking little fish and ruining the fishing for others – like us!"

The week-end came and because of the fretting children, Jeremy's mother allowed him to telephone Herman Gordon; to ask if and when they could expect to go fishing and swimming again. It was Moira Gordon who answered the telephone.

"Hello?"

"Oh! Is Mister Gordon at home please?" The youthful voice sounded very eager.

"Who is it calling?"

"It is Jeremy; Mister Gordon takes us fishing and that!"

"Oh, yes! No Dear, he is out working, can I help you?"

"We-ell, me and Gerard were just wondering when he is taking us fishing again – could you ask him please?"

There was a little pause, and then Moira said.

"Now he did mention something about that – how old are you Dear?"

"Huh? Me. I am ten – I will be eleven soon and Gerard is ten too, I am older but. His birthday is two weeks after mine."

"And Mister Gordon tells me that you are both very good boys – not cheeky – and obedient!"

"We try to be good – our parents will kill us if we're not – and Mister Gordon says we are well-mannered. Is he going to take us fishing again Missus Gordon, please?"

There was another pause, and then Moira answered as if still cogitating.

"He can not go anywhere this week-end, he and two other officers are on special duties. But he did leave me to make some arrangements for next week-end!"

"Oh!" It was a disappointed exclamation. Moira went on.

"Would you two boys mind if I came along to watch and prepare lunch for you all – have a real picnic?"

There was no immediate answer due to the boy pondering this new prospect; then he drawled.

"Don't suppose so – I mean – Gerard probably will not mind."

There was a slight pause as Jeremy thought things over, and then he tremulously asked.

"Do you go fishing too?"

"Sometimes, but next week-end I shall not be fishing, Mister Gordon and I have something else in mind. Are you sure it is all right for me to join you, Jeremy?"

"Yes Missus Gordon, but Mister Gordon is a scrumptious cook you know!"

"Yes Dear, I know. Could I talk to your mum for a little bit please?"

"Yes'm!" Jeremy called her. "Mum – Missus Gordon wants to talk to you!"

Jeremy was having pins and needles as the two ladies conversed. Odd comments from his mother after they had introduced themselves had the youngster confused. He stared fixedly at his mother as arrangements were made.

"Oh yes, they would love that!" She agreed. "Of course, if it is not too much of a burden on you – I am sure Matt will agree – I will set it up with Gerard's folks. Yes, yes – oh – and thank you. Yes – okay – 'bye, and thanks, the boys will be delighted. I will make sure they are ready, goodbye once again!" She hung the telephone on its cradle and turned to her son with a mischievous twinkle in her eyes.

"Missus Gordon says there will be no fishing with Mister Gordon this week-end, he is very busy!"

"Yes Mum, I know, Missus Gordon told me."

"But" - his mother went on – "they would like to take you next week-end!"

She looked for some excitement.

Jeremy asked matter-of-factly.

"Which day Mum; Saturday or Sunday?"

"Both!"

Jeremy gave a wide-eyed stare at his mother, and then frowned.

"What do you mean Mum. Is he coming on Saturday and then again on Sunday?"

"No Dear. They want to take you and Gerard on a picnic when you go fishing and because it is at another place, Mister Gordon knows; they wanted to know if you would like to stay with them for the week-end. Just overnight on Saturday. Do you think you and Gerard would like that?"

"Wow – yes. But we do not know Missus Gordon, this is the first time I have met her – and what about my jobs – Gerard has to do jobs at home too; what about them?"

"Don't you worry about your work Saturday night and Sunday morning, your dad and I will manage. I will fix it up with Gerard's parents too. Now, are you sure you want to go? You have to be sure so I can arrange things!"

"Yes Mum. Can I ring Gerard and see if he wants to go, please?"

"Of course, but do not hang up, I have to talk to his mother!"

It only took a few minutes for the parents of both boys to agree and finalise the arrangements for the following week-ends activities.

Jeremy and Gerard first made their own plans for that Saturday's fun, seeing that they would not be fishing with Herman Gordon. They decided to ride their bicycles to a dam which was located at the boundary fence of both their properties. It was actually halved by the fence and happened to be quite a large dam that had redfin and a few terrapins stocking it. The main attractions for the boys though, were the yabbies which abounded in it. They would catch enough for all picnickers to use the next week-end on the fishing trip. The catch could be retained in a large holding vat that Jeremy's father had built near their barn; specifically for the purpose of having fresh bait ready at hand. When the boys arrived at their destination, they were dismayed to find two fifteen-year-old strangers already fishing there. The strangers had evidently cycled to the dam themselves, as two bicycles were lying just behind them. The strangers looked up as the ten-year-olds approached.

"Nick off, we were here first!" The plump one ordered.

"No! You nick off, this is our dam; we own the properties!" Jeremy informed.

The tall skinny youth stood up.

"Bull! Anyway, what are you going to do about it?"

He left his rod and swaggered to the smaller boys.

Jeremy reached into his fishing creel and extracted a cellular telephone.

"I will just ring my Dad, that's what!" He stated, very confidently. "Mum made me bring it, 'case of snakes!"

"Arrgh! We were only mucking about, don't ring up; can we stay and fish here?"

The big fellow asked. Jeremy looked at Gerard, who just shrugged.

"S'pose so, but do not leave any bits of broken line in the dam or around. It can cause the stock to lose a hoof!"

"Yeah, awright. Wot's ya names? I am Peter and that is Larry!"

They were told the younger boy's names and all settled down to their fishing.

After fishing fruitlessly for an hour, the two youths bid farewell, mounted their bicycles and rode off towards the river at the rear of the younger boy's properties. Jeremy and Gerard also caught no fish so settled into their quest for yabbies. In this, they were quite successful; catching in excess of thirty bait-sized ones. The larger yabbies they tossed back to increase the yield as they had been taught; for later. The boys returned home, happy with their days outing but pondering upon whom the strangers were and from where they may have come. As they were not locals, the boys surmised that they must be on a fishing trip with their folks, who were possibly camped by the river.

CHAPTER SEVEN

The Larrikins

The next day found the youngsters back at their peninsular. After their good haul of yabbies for bait, but still not having caught a fish, they had decided at church that Sunday morning; that the peninsular would be a very good way to spend the afternoon. When riding along the track of the peninsular, Jeremy spotted a land-rover with a bicycle rack on the back. It was partly hidden between two gums with shrubbery growing in between them. He pointed the vehicle out to his fishing companion.

"Must be a fisherman at our spot!" He declared.

"Maybe not!" Gerard hopefully offered. "There are lots of other spots along here to fish. He may be at one of them!"

A little further along, two men were whispering to each other. The boys rode past them before they noticed the men hidden from the approaching side.

"They do not have rods – wonder what they are doing?" Gerard queried, dubiously. Jeremy rode behind some bushes and dismounted from his bicycle.

"What is up, are we going to spy on them?" Gerard asked an evil glint in his eyes.

"No – I am worried; I do not think we should fish here. Remember what our parents said about strangers? I reckon we better nick off and fish somewhere else; maybe downstream!"

"Aw! We will be all right if we fish at our usual spot. If they stay here we will be okay up at the end!" Gerard pushed. "Come on, keep riding!" He mounted and rode off. Jeremy followed.

"Hey! Jeremy – Gerard – be quiet and come here!"

The voice which suddenly came from the right was urgently whispered, but the boys recognised Herman Gordon's voice.

"Hi Mister G-!!?"

"Shhh!" The man whispered. The boys came and Herman whispered for them to be silent.

"Did you see two men as you came here?" He asked.

"Yes, they were not fishermen. We passed them before we saw them." Jeremy answered.

"They are my men. Both are Game Wardens like me. We are trying to trap some illegal line-netters. I want you boys to ride back as if you are still looking for a fishing spot – go upstream – you will find my four wheel drive there; that is a good spot. Stay there and fish, will you do that for me?"

"Yes Mister Gordon." Both boys did as was asked of them.

After about an hour fishing during which time the pair caught five redfin between them, Herman Gordon returned with his two companions. They all carried fishing gear, which included drum and line nets. The three struggled under their huge loads.

"Thank goodness for that, a job well done boys!" Herman said to his assistants as they began loading the tackle into his vehicle.

"Wow – look at all that stuff, gee, wouldn't you catch some rippers with that?" Gerard noted.

Herman cast a very severe eye at the boy, and then called both over to him.

"Do you boys know what this netting is?" He asked. Jeremy answered.

"I think those barrels are used to catch fish!"

"No Jeremy. The barrels float the nets across the river. There are drums made of netting floating below in the water and they trap the fish. They are very illegal because the fish do not stand a chance to get away and the people who use these, sell the fish commercially. They bleed the river of fish and trap all sorts of illegal things - like terrapins and platypus. The terrapins and platypus drown because they are like us, they need to surface for air. You would not like to be trapped underwater in a net, would you?"

"No Sir! Did you catch the men responsible?"

"Yes, do you remember the man who was fishing with you the second time we met?" Herman asked.

"Yes Mister Gordon."

"Well, he was one of the two men we caught. I was keeping an eye on him when I came across you two boys." Gerard asked a question.

"What happens to the men when you catch them? Do you arrest them?"

His blue eyes were wide with wonder.

"Yes. Just until we charge them with illegal netting and confiscate their gear. We make them sign for all the gear we take and they have to pay a fine. If they do not pay it, then they may go to jail!"

The boys were introduced to the other officers and just as the vehicle was about to leave; Jeremy asked.

"What if they had their kids with them; do they get fined too?"

"Ha!" Herman laughed with his deep guttural tone. "No young man, not unless they were actually laying the lines. It is always the adults. You see, the current is swift in most rivers – or at least – quite strong, and it is very hard for children to set the lines. Although these men did have teenage boys with them; they came from fishing elsewhere on their bicycles, as we let the men go!"

"Two big boys on bikes were at our dam yesterday!" Gerard chipped in.

"Oh, was one short and plump and the other tall and skinny?" Herman asked.

"Yes!" Jeremy replied for Gerard.

"Well, if you find they have done any damage, we have their addresses!"

Herman began to drive off again, when Gerard called out.

"Wait Mister Gordon, please!"

The vehicle stopped and Herman leaned out.

"Yes Gerard, what is it?" The boy fidgeted, a little embarrassed.

"Is it true that you are having us staying at your house next week-end; to take us fishing?" Herman smiled.

"Oh. What gives you that idea?" Gerard and Jeremy frowned.

"My mum said Missus Gordon told Jeremy's mum that we were! Isn't it true then?" Herman laughed.

"If my wife said you are coming to my place, then it must be true. Why, have you changed your minds; don't you want to come now?"

"Oh yes, we do, we do, but you did not seem to know about it!"

Herman grinned expansively as he admitted.

"No, I did not know about it, I have been working all day; when did my wife ask your mum?"

He strained his neck around to see the boy who was a little behind Gerard.

"Just this morning Sir, I rang to see when you were letting us fish at your spot again and Missus Gordon asked us to stay over next Saturday night!"

"Well, if that is what Missus Gordon wants and you wish to stay – hey – that is wonderful. I will be glad to have you two be with us for the week-end. That is great; we will have heaps of fun!"

"Thank you Mister Gordon, we will be good, we promise!" Jeremy declared.

They waved their goodbyes as the four wheel drive departed.

. . . .

Joey Gruntz and Lance Gurnell had completed their community work orders. Both were still fuming over the two brats who caused their downfall and they vowed to 'get even' with the 'snotty-nosed' little blighters; as lance called them. It was the first time that the tall

41

city boy had dared venture back to visit his country friend. Joey too, had been forced to keep away from the little lads – by court order – however, that meant nothing to the bully. But like all bullies, he did stay away from them until he had the backing of his mate.

"How d'ya reckon we can make up for what the snivelling little rotters did to us?"

Joey asked. Lance was in a like dilemma.

"Dunno! I been talking to some 'a me mates in the city, an' they reckon we orta just scare the devil outa them. Dunno how, but I don't reckon that's good enough; what we orta do is poison their rotten apple orchard!"

"Hey! That's an idea, why don't we? We can do it at night and they won't know who did it!" Joey became alert.

"Nah! It is too much trouble and anyway, we don't know how to do it. We gotta think 'a somethin' what'll dish the kids; they are the ones we want, they dobbed us in!"

"Yeah!" Joey agreed. "Let's think of something diabolical!"

The larrikins strolled about the outskirts of the small country township, as they hatched up plots and plans. Most of their thoughts were either too trivial to suit their purpose, or so outlandish as to be impracticable. The youths eventually arrived at the sports oval and commented on the fact that repairs to the pavilion, were coming on quite well.

"Ay, why don't we burn the rotten thing down?" Lance suggested. Joey sadly shook his head.

"No, that's too obvious. I mean – it's the first day you are back in town and it burns down? They will send us to prison!"

"Yeah, I s'pose!" Lance concurred.

It was the same Sunday that Gerard and Jeremy had seen Herman Gordon and his men confiscate the drum net fishing gear. Jeremy had dutifully finished his evening jobs and was belatedly catching up on his homework, in his room. His parents were quietly reading in the lounge room, and Karen, Jeremy's little sister, had been put to bed. The household was very peaceful and quiet. Sam and Bluey, the household pets who were also the sheep and cattle dogs, were standing at their kennels, sniffing the air and uttering barely audible growls. They had scented something which was unfamiliar. Both kelpies ran up and down the length of their runner leads.

The causes of their interest were the two youths who were out of sight but silently creeping towards the house. They were hiding behind the barn, having left their old wreck of a car by the entrance gate of the property. Both had come the seven hundred and fifty metres from that gate to the barn on foot. The two did not want their visit announced. Being country bred, Joey knew the breeze would carry their scent to the farm animals. He advised his city friend of this fact; so it was that the two came from down-wind as best they could manage. Their plan was to steal Jeremy's fishing tackle out of the shed where he kept it, and ride back to the car on his bicycle. Then they were going to visit the other boy's home and do likewise. They planned to throw the lot into the river and so exact revenge upon the youngsters, however, their plans depended upon not being seen. It was imperative that they got clean away on both occasions. The youths quietly crept into the storage shed. Lance wheeled Jeremy's bicycle out and awaited Joey. Joey accidentally rattled the fishing gear, causing the dogs to snarl. Both youths stood still, trying not to breathe too heavily.

The dogs settled down again. Easing him and the fishing tackle out of the shed, Joey silently closed the shed door. The thieves hurriedly quit the area and hastened to their vehicle. Lance tried to 'dink' Joey with his armful of stolen goods but they tangled and fell over. The noise put the two dogs to barking. Joey and Lance ran helter skelter, Lance running beside the small bicycle. As they reached the car, the back door of the house opened and Jeremy's father went to quieten his dogs. He shone a torch about but could see nothing amiss. Matt searched about the back yard in the dark, his torch flitting hither and yon. He could see nothing out of place. He saw the shed door was closed so made his way to the barn. It too, was secure, as were the domestic stock. Again he returned to the dogs. Their eyes were focussed towards the front entrance to the property but Matt could see no movement. Nothing stirred, so he gave each of his dogs a final pat, and then returned to the house. Yvonne was awaiting him.

"What was it dear?" She asked.

"Oh, I don't think it was anything much; perhaps a fox after the poultry I suppose. Let us get back inside and relax love!"

They settled down to their reading once again. Peace came to their happy little world. Jeremy entered the lounge room.

"I finished my homework Mum – did I hear Sam and Bluey barking?"

"Yes Jeremy. Your Dad had a look; he thinks it was only a fox. Get to bed Dear, it is getting late; we will be up in a minute to tuck you in – hoppit!"

"Yes Mum."

Gerard's folks did not have such a large farm as his playmate's parents. About two thirds the size, but as he ran very few stock - just enough to keep the winter growth in order; there was no need for a larger property. His main income came from his vineyard and vegetable crops. He also cultivated a few flowers to supply the local florist. When the youths had put their stolen goods into the car, they sensibly sat and waited, watching the house with interest. As the back porch light was switched off after the door closed; the youths felt safe to quietly depart. They drove the few kilometres to the next door neighbour's farm, without headlights shining. As before, the vehicle was left at the front entrance gate to the property. The two stole towards the outhouses. Gerard had a pet dog too. Rover was in his dotage and was almost deaf; however his sense of smell was still most acute. Sometimes in the colder weather, he was allowed to sleep in the laundry, which was one of the back rooms of the rather large, rambling old homestead. More often than not, Rover slept on an old sofa on the back verandah. Rover did not see or hear the robbers as they ransacked the out-houses, seeking Gerard's fishing tackle. Unknown to them, it was stored in the house. Lance found the boy's bicycle and began to walk it back to the car. Joey, on the other hand was empty-handed; in desperation he grabbed a small saddle which was hanging in the bicycle shed. The surcingle clattered against a hay fork which was also hanging upon the wall. The noise was enough to have Rover come to investigate. When the old hound came close to the disturbance, his keen nostrils picked up the scent of strangers.

"Growff – growff – growff."
He boomed with his deep chesty bark. Joey found the saddle too awkward and rattling to run with it, the thing restricted his swift flight. Joey threw the saddle to the ground and hastened after Lance. Before they reached their vehicle, a motor approached and stopped at the cattle grid. It was Gerard's father, returning from a meeting. He shone his trouble-light all over the dilapidated vehicle; recognising it immediately. The light was extensively flashed about his paddocks and a fleeting glimpse of the two youths and a bicycle was seen.

The few bushes either side of the driveway afforded some cover but the game was up. Gerard's father recognised Jeremy's bike which was often seen at his back door. He also remembered Jeremy's fishing tackle, when he saw it in the car.

"Joey Gruntz! I know you are there, come here and bring my son's bicycle with you!"
He ordered.

CHAPTER EIGHT

A Fun Week-end

The younger boys were not told of the attempted robberies or who it was that were to blame. Both families deemed it better to just replace the bicycles and fishing gear, without causing undue stress upon their off-spring. The youths were allowed to go with only a severe tongue lashing and the knowledge that their actions would be reported to the local constabulary. Joey and Lance, still stinging from the previous fines and community work orders; became worried by the act that this second offence, could cause a prison term. The pair decided to leave the younger boys alone; the youths seemed to come off second best every time they bothered the boys and their families. Arrangement had been made for Herman to pick up both boys from Jeremy's house, as it was closer to Herman's home. Gerard was driven over by his parents and the whole family of each boy, was there to see them off; on what well may turn out to be the most exciting week-end of their lives. The two youngsters were bubbling over with excitement. They saw to their morning chores a little earlier than usual and Jeremy had trouble coaxing the milkers to give. Eventually everything was accomplished that was expected of them and the two little lads checked their baggage. Yes! Swimming gear, pj's and tooth brushes were all packed; including a change of clothing and wet weather cover-alls, just in case.

Percy and Grace Lonard proudly watched their only son as he exuberantly clambered into the back seat of Herman Gordon's four wheel drive; as did Matt and Yvonne Purcell, after cuddling their Jeremy. All waved farewell and the great outing began. Leanne, Gerard's older sister, sadly waved to her brother, bemoaning the fact that she never went anywhere; and wasn't it about time she did? Her father squeezed her shoulders, saying

"Never mind dear, your turn will come and remember how often you have been sleeping over at your school friend's places? It was only a few weeks ago that you stayed at Jenny Barnes' home, with Flossie, wasn't it?" Leanne nodded.

"Yes, I suppose!"

"There Leanne, don't begrudge your little brother an outing, you have had lots more than he has!"

"Time for a cuppa everyone, come inside please!" Yvonne called as she led the way.

Herman and his happy group disappeared from sight along the riverside road. Herman and Moira had slight smiles upon their faces as they motored along. The unfamiliar sounds of two very excited youngsters eagerly chatting and surmising the week-ends activities, was music to their ears.

"I do believe we are going to thoroughly enjoy this week-end dear."

Moira softly cooed to her husband.

"You should Love, these little blokes will not cause us any problems and they promised to behave properly, so we should have a wonderful, happy time; eh boys!" Herman boomed.

"Yes Mister Gordon!" Both boys chorused.

"Er – excuse me – but where are we going?" It was Jeremy who asked, Gerard became attentive for the answer too.

"Portman's Creek, it is a lovely ice-cold trout stream up to those ranges you can see from here. Your father used to fish there Jeremy and when I checked the arrangements for you boys to come for the week-end, he reminded me about it. Gosh! I have not fished there for years, so it will be a great thrill for me too. We will fish for a couple of hours, and then have a picnic lunch. Does that sound exciting?"

"Wow! I'll say!" Came from Gerard.

"My word!" Came from Jeremy.

The happy group duly arrived at their destination at nine in the morning. Tall eucalypts and tree ferns were abundant as was the bracken fern, which served as great cover for the myriads of wild-life in the area. The sound of the elusive little bell-birds with their whiplash peal, gave the scene a peaceful tranquillity the likes of which one must experience to fully appreciate. But to the merry travellers, the gurgling ripple of the clear and freezing trout-stream; was the manna from heaven to which they aspired to the most.

"Oh! Isn't this a divine place to fish?" Moira gushed. "Come boys, let us get the gear out, who would like to fish with me?" She asked. Jeremy volunteered.

"Good lad Jeremy." Herman praised. "You come and fish with me Gerard; we are going to catch many more fish than Missus Gordon and Jeremy; aren't we?"

"I'll say!" That worthy concurred.

"You can, but we are only catching the big ones; aren't we Missus Gordon?" Jeremy bragged.

"You are so right little man, come and help me find the best fishing spot!" Moira led the way.

As the four sat and fished, Jeremy whispered to Moira.

"Are there big brown in here or are there just rainbow trout.

"Not JUST rainbow trout. Mister Gordon tells me that there are two and three pound rainbow trout in here, almost two kilo trout are big ones you know; and there are some brown trout too!"

"Gee! I reckon they should bite really soon, don't you? I mean, this is a very quiet spot!" Jeremy was a little wistful. Moira patted his knee.

"Be patient, we will get a bite soon!"

"I've got a bite!" Gerard whispered. "My cork's taken down!"

"Give him some line – okay – strike now!" Herman returned the whisper.

Moira and Jeremy heard the drip of water from Gerard's net and a splash as the fish made a final desperate bid for freedom. Gerard landed the first catch; it was about one and a half pounds of nice rainbow trout. He proudly dispatched it with a sharp blow to the head with his fishing knife, and then bled it. The fish safely in his creel, the boy rebaited to try and add to his catch. Moira landed the next rainbow trout. It was almost identical to Gerard's catch.

When the time came for lunch, all had bagged good catches. Herman had only two fish but one of these was the grand daddy of them all, a huge brown that was not a match for the wily old fisherman. The boys drooled over the lovely big fish.

"Gee! I wish I caught that one!" Gerard moaned.

"Me too!" Came from a jealous Jeremy.

Moira left the cleaning of her catch to her husband while she washed her hands in warm soapy water, and then prepared the picnic lunch. All of the hungry fisher folk eyed the scrumptious spread eagerly.

"I can see chicken slices, eggs and corned beef – and – and lollies!"

Jeremy stated triumphantly.

"And cheese too, with pretzels – wow!" Gerard added.

"You can not eat until you have washed your hands properly boys!" Moira said. "In that bowl of hot water on the fold-up table by the car – hoppit!"

As the quartet sat upon the blanket spread for the purpose and tucked into the goodies laid out on the table cloth, which they surrounded; Moira had cause to comment.

"My oh my, aren't we a happy little family – anyone for iced lemonade?"

"Oooh yes please!" Both boys keenly answered.

"Just tea for me thanks Love." Herman said, helping himself to the pot at hand.

"Cake or lollies?" Moira asked.

Two little boys did not answer immediately, and then Gerard awkwardly and almost inaudibly whispered.

"Could we have both please?"

"Of course Dear, but do have the cake first!"

"Yes'm."

Having caught enough fish for all three families, it was decided that they had their quota. The catch was stored in the huge ice-box which Herman had securely and permanently under a heavy canvas, in the loading area of his four wheel drive. Everything packed up neatly and all replete from a very tasty and filling lunch; the foursome once more set off on their journey.

The excited youngsters again queried. 'Where were they off to now?'

"More fishing?" Jeremy added, hopefully.

"No lads." Herman's deep tones were modulated; it was difficult for him to whisper properly.

"We have to travel a few kilometres and then when we reach my sister's house, we can all go swimming!" He looked briefly over a shoulder to witness the reaction on his little guests' faces.

"Has your sister got kids our age?" Jeremy tentatively queried.

"Not at home Jeremy, they have all grown up and have their own young families. My sister lost her husband years ago, so now she lives alone. I am positive she would love to hear youngsters splashing in her swimming pool again. She has had it serviced especially for you. There is still a fair way to go, so I would like you two boys to just relax in your seat-belts and try to get some rest – will you do that?"

"Yes Mister Gordon, we'll try!" Gerard led the way and closed his eyes.

The boys awoke when the car rattled over a cattle grid.

"Are we home yet Dad?" Gerard sleepily asked.

"He's not your dad, dopey! That is Mister and Missus Gordon." Jeremy giggled.

"Oops, sorry!" An embarrassed youngster apologised.

"Yes you duffer" Moira put in. "But don't you fret dear, we would love to have been your parents!"

Jane de Lune was a buxom lady who gushed over the children as they alighted from her brother's vehicle. She was waiting at the front door with a quite expectant look upon her homely features. After embracing her brother and sister-in-law; she set her eyes upon the two little boys who had come to visit.

"My oh my - what nice little boys – do come and give Auntie Jane a hug!"

She reached out and held them to her sides, a firm hand upon each boy's shoulder.

"Just call me Aunt Jane boys, because Missus de Lune is a mouthful, I know. Oh it is nice to have you bring my relations up – they needed an excuse for coming – so I have to thank you for that! Please, do come inside and we will get a drink into us and make ourselves comfortable!"

Jane held the wire door wide as they passed through. Moira led the entourage into the dining-kitchen area. The boys politely sat as the adults caught up with each other's news, the while they prepared or served some refreshments. Both boys casually gawked about this new environment. After many preliminary questions and answers were satisfied and all had finished their refreshments; Jane once more centred her attention upon her two small guests.

"My word, you boys have been so quiet and polite, what say we go up to your room? Come on lads, I will show you where you will sleep tonight and perhaps you might like to change into your swimming trunks – while you are there – anyone for a swim?"

"Ooh yes please!"

Quiet voices could be heard emanating from within the boy's temporary quarters; as Jane returned to her kin.

"Jeremy and Gerard are changing to go to the pool. Anyone else interested?" Jane queried.

"No Jane, not for me thanks. You and I can sit and chat. Herman, are you going swimming?" Moira asked. Herman pouted before replying.

"I do not really feel like a swim but I suppose someone had better keep an eye on the boys. I shall go and change, watch them for me please!"

The boys played, splashed and swam for an hour as their large guardian sat beneath the shade of an awning; the while he enjoyed the sight of his little friends frolicking in the large pool. The happy faces and exuberant laughter of the agile children, gave Herman a strange feeling of exaltation; foreign to his usual activities. There emerged from his inner being, a fatherly impulse which brought a warm cloak of liking – no! It was love – Herman was becoming very attached to these wonderful little boys and a strong yearning began to develop, which urged him to desire a family of his own. He resolved to broach the subject to his Dear Moira, once they were abed.

"Hey Mister Gordon, please come in with us!" Jeremy called.

"Yes, you can throw us about and we can dive off your shoulders!"

Gerard put his weight behind his pal's request.

"I do not feel like a swim, boys." Herman frowned.

"If you don't come in we will splash you!" Jeremy sang.

"Oh dear, I suppose I had better come in then before I get wet!" Herman quipped.

He splashed heavily in between the two unsuspecting youngsters who attempted to evade the situation. To their gleeful shrieks was added the impetus and strength of the huge man, as he carefully cast them aside. They swam back for more.

For half an hour Herman frolicked with the children. He left the pool to cries of dismay from both boys; when Moira called him out for a cuppa.

"Sorry lads, I need to replenish my energy; you have worn me out!"

Moira set their tray on the pool-side table, so all three adults could keep an eye on the boys; the children rested from their own exertions and sat upon the exit steps from the pool; to relive the enjoyment.

Jane and Moira sat idly chatting as Herman joined them after having dried himself.

"You seemed to be rather energetic dear!" Moira stated.

"Yes Love. I get a real kick out of making the little blokes happy. It is a change from forever dealing with adults. I can really let my hair down and relax – drop my guard if you will – and I find it a type of therapy; you know? Jove but I feel good right now. I do believe these little lads are making me feel young again!" He leaned across and gave Moira a huge kiss, saying

"Did I tell you how much I love you? I think I should take you in my arms and jump in to the pool with you!"

"Don't you dare?" Moira called in mock alarm, "or you will jolly well go without dinner tonight!"

"Ah dinner, my word but now that you mention it, I am quite hungry. I could eat you Love!" Herman nibbled at her ear.

"Herman!" Moira laughed as she tried feebly to avert her man. "Not in front of the children!"

CHAPTER NINE

The Fairgrounds

After the evening meal, two quite tired little boys were bedded down. Each of the adults came in to wish the youngsters goodnight. Jane placed a chair between the twin beds, at the foot of them, so that she could see the boy's faces and they could look into hers.

"Anyone for a bedtime story?" She coyly asked. "Or are you boys too big to bother?"

Both Gerard and Jeremy looked sheepishly at each other, before Jeremy begrudgingly stated.

"Well, we are getting to be big you know, but I have not heard a bedtime story for yonks. What is it about?"

"The story is about the legend of the earth tremors!" Jane answered, and then began.

"This is the story of Baluti Tanana. Baluti Tanana was a great and fearless warrior in the remote part of the Australian outback. Although Baluti was a great warrior, he was also a very experienced fisherman. When his tribe were hungry, they could always rely upon Baluti to catch enough fish to feed them all. One time there came a great drought to the land and all of the water holes dried out. There was no water to be had and all the fish left floundering were taken by the birds and other wildlife. The tribe was afraid they would starve and die. In desperation, the tribal chief ordered Baluti to go forth and find food for the tribe, as he was the best fisherman and the greatest warrior of all; who could fight his way over the dry land and save the tribe. Baluti walked for days but could find no water, therefore no fish. One day, Baluti came to a dry waterhole and decided to dig for water. After a day of hard digging, Baluti dug so deeply that he fell through the hole into an underground river. Oh joy! The fishing was so good that Baluti caught enough fish to feed the tribe until the drought should break. But he could not reach the hole high above him and there was no way to get the fish out and take them back to his starving tribe. So the tribe moved away to find food and water elsewhere. Baluti was left to wander underground seeking a way out, so that he could save his people. If you put your ear to the ground, you may hear the rumble of Baluti as he roams the underground river, calling for his people to come and get the fish and rescue him. But they never come and Baluti is still roaming until this day!"

Jane noticed that Gerard had nodded off and Jeremy was heavy-lidded. She kissed their foreheads as she whispered.

"Good night Dear!"

"Mmpfft!" The boy answered, and then fell asleep.

Jane joined her brother and sister-in-law, as they sipped a warm drink in the lounge-room.

"My word Sis! You look a happy little soul; is that contented clucking I hear?"

Her brother impishly asked.

"Yes, I think it well could be. Is there any chance that you might trundle off home tomorrow and leave them here? They are such sweet little chaps. I am so pleased you brought them with you – I feel like a mum again!"

Jane sat with them as Moira poured her a cup of tea.

"Home made shortbread Jane?" Moira asked.

"Ta! I think you will have to bring them to visit again one day – see if their folks can do without them for a week and we will all have a holiday together. I enjoyed hearing them splash and play in the pool today. What say Hermie – in the school holidays – could you arrange it?" Jane's eager heart tugged at her brother.

"They may not wish to come you know and anyway, it is possible that they already have other plans arranged!" Herman answered.

Moira had been sipping quietly as they spoke. She muttered, almost inaudibly to herself.

"I'd love that!"

"Hello, ganging up on me again." Herman grinned, and then deliberated. "Suppose I could arrange my work around it, Pat is looking for extra time; he could fill in for me quite easily. It all does depend upon the parents of the little chaps and of course, the boys themselves. I won't mention anything about it to them until I have spoken to their parents. If I ask the boys now, they may feel obliged to answer in the affirmative – we don't want to embarrass them!"

"What is in store for tomorrow Hermie, are you still going to the fair?" Jane asked.

Herman looked keenly at Moira as he answered.

"Oh, but of course. I promised Moira a re-enactment of our engagement – in the tunnel of love – that is the main reason for this trip! Did you think it was just for the boys?"

"Herman!" Moira expostulated. "You remembered – you remembered our ninth wedding anniversary. Oh, I should have known – you proposed to me in the tunnel of love!"

She leaned across to kiss him. Herman responded.

"I love you more dearly now than I did then, Dear!" They embraced fondly.

Jane arose, saying.

"That is my cue, I am off to bed. I will take this tray with me and do the dishes while you two love-birds carry on – goodnight!"

She left the room and closed the door after her. Moira and Herman were quite unaware of the noises in the kitchen as Jane washed up and tidied; before she retired. Herman gently squeezed his wife as he planted loving kisses upon her neck and cheeks, then firmly stopped her happy sighs with a full, warm kiss upon her lips. When they parted slightly to regain their breath; he whispered.

"What do you think of the children Dear?"

"Huh?" Her shock at the change of subject was evident. "What have the children to do with our anniversary?" Moira asked in awe.

"Do you enjoy having the boys about, Love?" Herman persisted.

"Why, yes! They are nice little chaps and I -!! Herman, you are not thinking of us having a family?"

"Why not? I think it is time – I am getting quite fond of them – I shall miss them when they have to go. Moira Dear, my Darling, we are quite settled now and a family of little ones like these two appeals to me very much. A man needs a son about and would you not like a daughter to teach cooking and sewing?"

Moira softened as she gazed lovingly deep into her man's keen eyes.

"Yes! I know you will make a wonderful father for our children. If you think it is time now to start; let us work at it. Oh Herman, I do love you so!"

They retired for the night, that happy anniversary night!

Sunday morning found Jane up early and trying not to clatter too much as she traipsed around the kitchen, preparing breakfast for her welcome guests. As she turned sharply to reach for the kettle which began to shriek its warning; Jane was surprised to see young Jeremy standing in the doorway, rubbing his eyes.

"Do I have to feed the chooks or something?" He asked.

"No Dear, we do not need to run chickens so close to the city. Tell you what though, if you hop back into bed, I shall bring a tray up and you can have brekkie in bed – would you like that?" Jane raised her eyebrows expecting the answer that she got.

"Ooh, yes please!" Jeremy raced back to the bedroom.

By the time the children had finished their breakfasts, Herman was up and dressed. He poked his head into the boy's bedroom and asked.

"Did you sleep well Lads?"

"Yes Mister Gordon." They both replied.

"What are we doing today?"

It was Gerard who was inquisitive.

"If you put on your fishing clothes, we may be able to get an hour's fishing in at Aunt Jane's creek, down the back of the property here. We may only catch blackfish or an eel, but it is fishing. We have to be back by ten so we can shower and be ready for church. Anyone interested?"

The fishing was poor. Both boys had a few nibbles but they were unrewarded. Herman caught an eel, which he knew his sister loved to eat. The three hurried back to the house and got themselves ready for church. Each of the adults, in their own way, felt as if they were a family as they attended the service. Part of the deal in allowing the children to go on this excursion, was that they did not miss the Sunday Religious experience.

At lunch after the service, both boys sat wide-eyed as Herman explained what was in store for the afternoon.

"It is only a twenty minutes run through the suburbs to the fairground, so ---!"

"Fairground?" Jeremy butted in. "Are we going to the fairground?"

Gerard was suddenly alert as he too, eagerly and expectantly looked to Herman for confirmation of this wonderful surprise.

"Yes! Is everybody happy about that?"

"Ooh, I'll say!" And "Yes sir!" Were the replies.

Three very contented adults wandered aimlessly about the fairgrounds, in the leisurely pursuit of the two exuberant ten-year-olds, who scooted from one attraction to the other. Jane had taken it upon herself to keep a protective eye on the boys as Herman and Moira re-lived their honeymoon and the proposal; nine or so years since. Jane had her camera and was eagerly taking snapshots of her kin, as well as of the happy little boys who were her welcome guests. Gerard and Jeremy were racing each other in Dodgem Cars, when Jeremy was heavily jolted from the rear. His happy chuckles turned to fear when he glanced behind to see who the aggressive one was. He found the leering face of Lance, only a metre from him.

"Gerard! Get him, it's Joey's friend!" He shrieked.

Gerard swung full circle to come up behind the bully's dodgem and rammed it fiercely. Jeremy used the respite to likewise circle and attack from the side. First one and then the other jolted the big city lout and because of the double attack, he was unable to circle himself.

"You rotten little twerps!" He snarled. "Just wait 'til you get out – I'll flatten you both!"

Then the power was switched off and all Dodgems came to a standstill.

"Run Gerard – run!" Jeremy urgently called to his pal. They ran. Aunt Jane was awaiting the boys as they made for the exit doors from the Dodgem arena.

"Hold up boys, what is the rush?" She cautioned.

Lance Gurnel came to an abrupt halt in his pursuit of the two youngsters. Herman's sister was not so less massive than her brother, and quite wisely Lance satisfied himself with shaking a fist at the boys. Jane gave the lout a most severe look which bode ill for him, should Lance persist in his endeavours to get at her charges.

The boys enticed Aunt Jane to join them in a ride on a Whirly-gig. To the energetic children it was a rather lack-lustre and sedate experience, however for Aunt Jane; the ride was quite exciting enough. More so since she had the boys under her wing and was privy to their happy chuckles and glowing faces. Her camera snapped incessantly – she was enjoying herself immensely. Moira and Herman were still re-living his proposal to his wife with a child-free reminisce through the Tunnel of Love, on the River Boats ride. Came mid-afternoon and it was time to return home. Two happy little lads chatted ceaselessly in the rear of Aunt Jane's sedan, as she drove her guests back to her house. Herman and Moira were still re-living their engagement and honey-moon beside her in the front seat. The journey from the fairground seemed to take no time at all and before long, all were enjoying a cuppa before saying their farewells. The boys had partaken of fairy floss, drinks and ice-cream at the entertainment centre; so were sent to their room to pack their meagre belongings. Jane was dutifully thanked by the boys with a sloppy kiss upon her cheek. She responded by asking them not to forget her and please come back another time. A parting snapshot of the lads happily waving from her brother's four wheel drive; had her dewy eyed. The visitors departed on the final leg of their happy week-end holiday. The journey home was made in contented solitude as both Moira and Herman were happy with their lot. Their temporary extended family were sound asleep in their seat-belts; after a hectic and quite fulfilling week-end of excitement. The families of both boys were inundated with the exploits of their off-spring and most happy to have them back home.

Two very contented adults made their way home, loaded with farm produce and the thanks of the two families, ringing in their ears.

"Did you find the strain of two very energetic youngsters tiring Dear?" Herman asked.

Moira squeezed her man's arm.

"On the contrary Herman, they are such adorable little chaps - I had a wonderful week-end. Oh, didn't Jane take to them though? I am rather looking forwards to another time like that. Children do liven one up, don't they?"

"Yes, I must ring their parents up in a week or so and see if we can make Jane happy during the school holidays!"

"Oh yes!" Moira agreed, then. "I am beginning to feel that maybe our very own family might not be such a bad idea – don't you?"

Herman smiled and stole a quick kiss as he eased the vehicle to the side of the roadway.

CHAPTER TEN

An Explosive Situation

For Jeremy and Gerard, the mundane tasks of the farming family came back to the fore. Many boring weeks of school and nights of homework became the norm once again. The only respite the two lads enjoyed, were the carefree fishing week-ends at their peninsular. They were not bothered by any of those people of the past months. Joey was only occasionally sighted upon the Sunday church times and his city friend, Lance; was not seen again since the advent of the day at the fairgrounds. Only once did the boys see the two fifteen-year-olds who were fishing from their dam; that was as Jeremy and Gerard were riding across the gravel road as they made their way to the peninsular. The youths waved to them from a passing car. The younger boys waved back. The fishing was not so good these days. One week-end the boys were forced to return home with empty creels. Only a few half-hearted nibbles rewarded them for a monotonous week-end of sitting by the riverside. Another week-end, they caught but three redfin and no trout. Gerard despondently suggested that they should go to Herman Gordon's secret spot.

"Maybe he will be there and will let us in!" Gerard urgently surmised.

"What if I ring up and ask him? I have his number here – I wrote it on my creel – just in case!" Jeremy said.

"My mum said we must not bother him unless it is an emergency!" Gerard cautiously warned.

"Yes, so did my dad. Won't hurt to ride there anyway, he just may be there!"

Jeremy became eager.

"Okay, let's!"

To their surprise when the two arrived at the cyclone wire gate, the lock was undone and the gate was slightly ajar.

"Told you, he is here!" Stated Gerard. "Let's go!" Jeremy was a little reticent.

"Wait Gerard, wait; something is wrong! I reckon someone has broken in to go fishing or something. Remember, Mister Gordon always locks the gate when he goes in; he never leaves the gate unlocked. Let us creep in carefully; I reckon those illegal net-fishers are there!"

"Gee! I hope they are, and then we will have an excuse to ring Mister Gordon!" Gerard whispered.

"Don't be daffy!" Jeremy ejaculated. "The fishing will be ruined if they are using the nets."

"Oh yeah! We better creep up and see who is there, just the same!"

Gerard was determined. Jeremy was not so sure.

"I think we should ring Mister Gordon and check up about the gate first; it might be Joey and Lance, they could be robbing the shack!"

Gerard was already through the gate and began riding towards the shack. It was about two hundred metres from the gate.

"Arrgh! Come on Jeremy, we can sneak up and check who is there; they won't see us if we are careful. Anyway, I bet it is just Mister Gordon!"

Jeremy was still not convinced but stayed with his pal. It was one of the strict rules laid down by his parents. They should always stick together and not roam away on their own. The inquisitive boys carefully rode their bicycles along the almost indiscernible track; ready to duck behind the covering shrubbery should flight be necessary. A surprise awaited them as the boys came within sight of the shack. The door was open but there was no sign of anybody about, nor was there any sign of a vehicle.

"Mister Gordon may have driven to the shed. Think we should go and see?" Jeremy asked.

"What if someone else is in the shack? They might be asleep!" Gerard suggested.

"I am going to ring Mister Gordon. If Missus Gordon answers, she will know if he is here!" Jeremy did so.

"Hello?" Missus Gordon's dulcet tones modulated through the receiver.

"It is Jeremy Purcell Missus Gordon, is Mister Gordon there please?"

"Why yes dear, how have you been? I will just go and get him for you!"

"Yes Jeremy, what can I do for you young man?" Herman boomed over the telephone.

"Mister Gordon, I hope you are not angry with us but we found your gate open and we thought you might be there –"

"What gate Jeremy, you don't mean the one to my shack do you?"

"Yes Sir. And when we rode up to the shack, the door is open, but there is no one about! What shall we do - should we look inside to see?"

"Gracious me no boy, not at all. Where are you now?"

Jeremy became a little worried by the man's words. He whispered as he urged Gerard to come and hide in the bushes.

"We are just at the edge of the clearing, near the track, hiding in the bushes. What do you want us to do?"

Herman made the boy promise that he and Gerard would stay exactly where they were, no matter who they saw and to remain hidden. He would come immediately, so the boys must wait fifteen minutes at least, until Herman arrived. It was a long fifteen minutes to the boys but they were obedient and did as they were bid by their mentor. Of a sudden, there came to their ears a huge explosion; it came from the river.

"Wow! What was that?" Gerard whispered eyes wide in alarm.

"I reckon whoever broke into the shack has stolen some of the explosives from the shed – gee, I hope Mister Gordon comes soon – I am getting scared!" Jeremy answered.

It was another ten minutes before the boys heard the stealthy approach of someone coming through the bushes.

"Here he comes Jeremy, Mister Gordon is coming, and he must have left his wagon by the gate!"

The boys rose to greet him, leaving their bicycles and fishing gear under the bushes where they had been hiding. They made their way to the person who was coming through the scrub.

It was not Herman Gordon!

Terrence Grail hastily dropped the bundles he was struggling with. Two potato sacks were dropped immediately, but a smaller bag was gently placed upon the ground before the smelly little man turned his attention to the boys.

"What are you boys doing here? This is private property, explain yourselves!" He demanded.

"No its not, this is council property and Mister Gordon is in charge. YOU are trespassing!" Jeremy stated with authority.

"Hey! Ain't you the brat what run me down with a horse?"

Terrence grabbed each boy by an arm and dragged them over to the shack. He roughly shoved the two inside and slammed the door shut behind him. The man raised an arm as if to strike Jeremy; the boy flinched away, retreating into the bedroom. Gerard attempted to follow his pal but was thrown firmly inside by Terrence, who placed a foot upon the boy's rear and straightened his leg; sending the blonde youngster sprawling over his dark-haired mate. The boys heard a chair being jammed against the door and the doorknob wiggled. They knew they were locked in and began to panic. "You'll stay there and rot for all I care!" Terrence snarled.

He slammed the entrance door of the shack and left. Jeremy and Gerard sat in silence, listening to the faint rustle as the smelly little man shuffled away.

"What will we do?" Gerard asked.

"Don't worry!" Jeremy assured him. "Mister Gordon will be here soon!"

Terrence returned to his sacks and after struggling to get the load settled over his shoulders, made his way along a game trail beside the river bank. He eventually came to the dividing fence, where he laid his load down. Sitting beneath a tree, he rested; knowing that he could squeeze through the hole where the restraining wires had been broken, so he could enter the council land easily. Being a vagrant, he had lived by the river for many months and had made such holes for easy ingress and egress. While Terrence rested he noticed the Game Warden's vehicle rush past. The man immediately scraped a hole out under a bush and buried the smaller sack, which held the explosives. Squeezing through the opening in the fence, he hurried away with his load of fish. Knowing all the game trails; he was soon off the normal fisher folk's tracks and lost in the shrubbery. He cackled to himself.

"Bet that smart Alec couple of kids get into trouble, breaking into the shack like that!"

Herman did as Jeremy surmised he would do and left his four-wheel-drive near the gate. He hurried to where the boys said they would be waiting. They were not there! He came across the bicycles and tried to whisper.

"Jeremy – Gerard – where are you?" receiving no answer, Herman made his way cautiously to the rear of his shack. He heard the boys talking inside. Quietly he unfastened the front door and crept to the chair. He heard an urgent whispering.

"He's back Gerard – get something to hit him with!"

Relieved, Herman called.

"It is all right boys; it is me – Herman – are you okay?"

At the same time he had the door opened. Jeremy came out first and wrapped his arms about his mentor's waist as he answered.

"Yes Mister Gordon, gee, we were scared he was coming back!"

"Who Lad, who were you afraid of?"

Gerard answered the question as he too, gave a big squeeze of relief to Herman.

"That smelly little man who robbed Mister Jenkins – he grabbed us and locked us in!"

"When he came we thought it was you." Jeremy enlightened.

"The rotter! Did he hurt you at all?" Herman asked a worried frown upon his brow.

"Only when he grabbed my arm and tossed me in the shack." Jeremy said.

"He kicked me in the bum!" Gerard snorted.

"Are you hurt?" Herman enquired.

"No – not really – it was more of a push."

"Where is he now, do you know?" He looked from one lad to the other.

"We heard him shuffle off towards the gate about ten minutes ago!" Gerard informed.

"And we heard a big bang – I think it was the explosives shed blowing up!" Jeremy said, wide eyed.

"What!" Herman expostulated. "Come with me lads!"

He led the way.

The explosives shack was still standing. Herman noted that the chain had been snapped by an iron bar which was left lying upon the ground. The lock too, was damaged and hung uselessly from the loop through which the clasp was secured.

"Came prepared." Herman pointed to the bar. "So it was obvious that he has been here before!"

They went into the building.

"Stay by the door boys, you are not allowed in here, it is too dangerous." Herman warned.

"Why?" Jeremy was interested.

"You could stand on a detonator or something and blow a leg off – or worse!"

Both boys froze where they were.

"Looks like a few detonators and half a dozen sticks of gelly are missing." Herman idly told himself.

"What sort of jelly, can you eat it?" Jeremy asked his brown eyes alight with wonder.

Herman smiled.

"No Jeremy, gelly is just a short name for gelignite; it is a very dangerous explosive. We need it for breaking rocks when road-making or for clearing blockages in the river; things like that!"

"Oh!"

"That man – Terrence I believe his name is – probably threw a stick into the river to stun the fish. They float to the surface and then it is just a matter of gathering them up; it ruins the fishing for weeks!"

"Wow! That must have been the bang we heard. How many fish do you reckon he got?" Gerard asked.

"You saw what he was carrying didn't you?" Herman looked to Jeremy for the answer, knowing he was more the instigator of the two boys; and the most observant.

"He had two potato sacks half full of something and a small canvas bag. He was very careful when he placed the canvas bag on the ground!"

"Must have stunned a couple of dozen fish by the sound of that!" Herman mused.

"What is a dozen Mister Gordon?" Gerard asked.

"Twelve – just two more than ten. Eggs are still sold by the dozen."

Herman ushered the boys out of the shed and secured it as best he could.

"Righto Lads!" He ordered. "Let us close my shack and I think you blokes had better get home. Bring your bikes and gear along and I will take you there!"

"Ah gee! But we haven't done any fishing yet!" Gerard grizzled.

Herman gave the boy one of his severe looks.

"The explosion has ruined the fishing, and anyway, that nasty man may be lurking about ready to grab you again. Your folks will not think I am responsible if I let you roam about after what has happened!"

A telephone call from his car to the parents of the boys had Herman drive directly to the small township. They stopped at the

Police Station, where the boys retold of their experiences. It was duly noted that Terrence Grail was the felon and a bulletin was put out for his apprehension. This time, he would not escape with a trivial sentence. But first he must be caught!

CHAPTER ELEVEN

Caught – and the Arrangements

Herman Gordon was dutifully doing his mid-week rounds of patrolling the known fishing and gaming areas of his protectorate. It had been a quiet week as the majority of people fishing, mostly came during the week-ends. There were many regulars who were pensioners or out-of-work idlers, who became well known to Herman and his aides; however, none were any cause for concern to the regulators and they always did the right thing. Catches of correct sizes were the only ones taken and the areas where they fished, on average, remained unlittered. It was with grave concern that Herman responded to a telephone call from his under-study, Pat. The man had come across those line-netters of their previous encounter; where the men were fined and fishing possessions confiscated. It was obvious that these men were again flouting the law, as Pat, from concealment, was watching a like occurrence being repeated. From whispered directions over the telephone, Herman was directed to the exact spot from which Pat was keeping an eye on the poachers. The officers watched the illegal activities for a few minutes, and then made themselves known to the two men who were hauling in the nets. Both dropped what they were doing and ran hastily to their land-rover. Herman noted that the rear number plate was missing, but he recognised the vehicle as the one from which the illegal netting of his previous arrest, was confiscated. He and Pat were almost upon the two men when an awful explosion behind them, tore at the bank of the river; uprooting a small shrub. The reverberation of the explosion echoed about the valley as mud, dust, rocks and clumps of grasses, rained down over the officers. The land-rover hastily departed, leaving Herman and Pat bereft of arrestees. Both men instinctively looked to the area of the disturbance for its cause. Herman could only guess that the man, who stole the explosives from his shack, was responsible. He let his fierce and angry gaze sweep the river banks on either side. Herman knew for whom he was searching – Terrence Grail – for it could be none other! The crashing of a body making haste through the scrub came to their ears. Both officers took off in pursuit and after a chase of some fifty metres, espied their quarry. With furtive glances behind, Terrence ran with the speed of a startled elk; albeit much more ungainly. He carried a small khaki shoulder bag which both pursuers recognised as council property – stolen from the explosives shed!

"Careful Pat, he still has explosives!" Herman warned.

The more powerful men were gaining valuable ground on Terrence as he reached the faint vehicle track. All heard the motor of the land-rover as it idled by, awaiting Terrence. He had no hope of reaching the vehicle, before the officers would overtake him. The vehicle drove off, leaving the vagrant abandoned. Terrence cried blue murder after his new acquaintances, who left him to his fate. The man took in hand a stick of gelignite from the khaki bag. Holding the explosive high overhead so the pursuers could not fail to see it, Terrence gently placed the bag at his feet.

"Stay put or I toss it!" He yelled at his pursuers, they halted.

"Be careful Terrence! That stuff may not be too stable." Herman warned.

"Then stand back and lemme go!" Terrence eyed the officers warily.

"Put the gelly down and you can go free!" Herman offered.

"You ain't kiddin'- ya won't renege'?" The vagrant queried.

"No – soon as you lay the stick down, you can go!" Herman assured.

Carefully Terrence placed the stick of gelignite on top of the khaki bag and while still keeping a wary eye upon his two pursuers; left the scene hurriedly. He disappeared amongst the shrubbery.

Pat gently placed the stick in the bag, checking first that the other items in it were not at risk of detonating. He carefully went back to the vehicles to place the bag in safety, the while he asked his immediate superior why Herman let the little vagrant go free.

"I know him from other nuisances he has caused. That is Terrence Grail, the bloke who robbed Jenkins' Store. He also bothered my little friends on two – no three – occasions now. I shall eventually catch up to him and exact my revenge; he is becoming too dangerous a man to let roam free in this district!"

Once again the officers confiscated the line nets of the poachers. These were old nets and almost useless, no doubt having been called into use, since the poachers' new nets were taken. Herman dutifully wrote down all the necessary details regarding the nets, the reason for their retention and a description of the poachers and their vehicle. Terrence Grail was also listed as a dangerous accomplice. The details of the wanted men were telephoned through to the local constabulary, with a special query upon the reason for a known felon, being at large. Meanwhile, Terrence had managed to make good ground and was well on the way to his isolated lean-to, which the hobo had used for a home over the past few months. He was cursing his new-found acquaintances who drove off and left him when he needed their assistance, and after he had provided them with the diversion which allowed them to escape. Consequently, the arrogant and thieving little man swore dire reprisals against those acquaintances. It was with mixed feelings that Terrence stumbled upon the errant pair. They were parked behind heavy shrubbery just off the roadway. Their land-rover was well hidden from view of the roadway but as Terrence came from the game trails which paralleled the river, it was more easily seen. He approached the vehicle cautiously. Both occupants alighted from the vehicle and went to him.

"Knew you'd find us!" One of them stated. "Waited 'specially for ya!"

"You did?" Terrence queried, dubiously.

"Sure. You gave us a chance to get away and we knew you'd come from this direction – just a matter of waiting. Hop in, we better scoot!"

"Crikey! Thanks, I was wanting to get away from here. Can you take me along the river a bit? Got a few things I have to pick up!" Terrence asked.

The men agreed. It was just a matter of five minutes and Terrence had a swag of goodies and personal effects, packed and stashed in the empty rear section of the land rover. A very happy vagrant was finally being taken from the district which seemed to have thwarted his designs, at every turning. Terrence had a very smug expression on his face as he thought of the swag of goodies, pilfered from farms houses and safely in his keeping. Towards the outskirts of the shire, the smug expression made a sudden dispersal as the three miscreants were brought to a stop by a police road block. Eventually the three were to pay for their felonies and Terrence was finally heavily convicted by the damning evidence in his possession. The poachers were also implicated as accessories to the fact, as well as being brought to bear regarding their illegal activities by the river.

. . . .

Herman Gordon was in urgent conversation with Matt and Yvonne Purcell, over a cup of tea and savoury sandwiches. The big man had arranged per telephone for a quick visit, to discuss a matter of great moment to he and his wife; consequently requesting that their meeting should be held when the youngsters were asleep. It was with some anticipation that the hosts awaited the gist of their new-found friend's interest in regard to their off-spring, for the matter of his visit would surely be in relation to their son; Jeremy. And so it proved.

"It is more for our benefit and the children's, that I make this suggestion – instigated, I might add – by my sister Jane. She just fell in love with the young fellows when they came to visit and she has missed youngsters in the house, since her own family grew up and went their ways. She does get lonely living by herself and she really is wonderful with children!"

Herman pushed his proposal with a reminder that the boys did have a great time and enjoyed their week-end away.

"Oh yes!" Yvonne noted. "Jeremy has spoken much of that week-end – especially at the fair – my word, both boys had a wonderful time. We do thank you for that!"

Matt absently nodded, concurring with his wife; his mind seemingly pre-occupied momentarily. Herman looked to him for his input.

"Of course, you may have family plans for the coming school holidays. It is just for the one week you know. Moira and I would love to have them along, providing they wish to come of course, but please do not let me influence you if you already have made other arrangements!"

Yvonne shook her head. "No, we must be here for the stock. We do not have anything in mind – er – do you dear?" She looked once again to Matt.

"Eh? No – no – I was fiddling with the idea of squeezing in a couple of days fishing with Jeremy. Naturally, the holidays will take a few weeks, so there is plenty of time for that! I believe if it is all right with Yvonne, and young Jeremy does show an inclination to want to go, I think that would be splendid for him!"

"It would give us a break too!" Yvonne added.

"So we have your approval?" Herman asked.

"Yes Herman, I know young Jeremy will be breaking his neck to accompany you and your family on whatever excursion you may have in mind. He hero-worships you, you know. He never seems to tire of re-living the exciting exploits that have eventuated over the past few months!" Matt reached out a friendly hand for Herman to grasp.

"I just do not seem to have the time to spend with the boy that I should, the farm and orchard demand so much of my time you know. I will definitely make some time to have a couple of quiet days fishing with our son, after he comes back – just to settle him down – now promise you will not over excite the boy!"

"I fear young Gerald will not be able to go this time Herman!" Yvonne informed.

"Oh?" Herman raised an eyebrow. "Is he ailing?"

"No, nothing like that, the two are very healthy specimens." Yvonne proudly said, shaking her head as she continued. "I was speaking with Grace at church last Sunday and she mentioned that her two may be going to their Nanna's over the holiday period; would you like me to ring her and make sure?"

A little of disappointment showed on Herman's face momentarily.

"Will that make any difference? Jane was so looking forwards to both boys romping in her swimming pool!"

"I will just check!" Yvonne picked up the telephone and rang her friend and neighbour.

Having had an urgent conversation with Grace over the telephone, Yvonne turned a sympathetic face to Herman. She elaborated on the snippets of replies she gave, that were obvious to those listening.

"Sorry Herman, Grace and Percy are having a break from the vineyard and gardens. They have his brothers and a sister exchange places so they can get away. Percy's family are going to live in and tend the place while they go on a much-needed holiday and the children are definitely off to their Nanna's place – sorry!"

"That is bad luck for young Jeremy; he will be lost without his cobber. You still do not mind him coming with us, even though he will be alone?"

Herman eyed the boys' parents speculatively.

"Not at all Herman, we appreciate you will look after Jeremy's interests as we would ourselves. Please rest assured that we have the greatest faith and confidence in you to protect our boy!" Yvonne gushed.

Matt nodded his concurrence, and then mused.

"What about Karen?"

"Karen?" It was an inspiration on the side-burner. "But of course! Jeremy loves his little sister, I am sure they would play well together. You don't think she is a little young to be away from me Dear; do you?" Yvonne worried.

"She is seven years old, I am sure a week will not adversely affect her, it may do her the world of good. Karen needs a change of environment too; part of growing up!" Matt asserted, then. "Anyway, she will have Missus Gordon and Missus de Lune. They would comfort her if she gets a little home-sick I feel sure, but of course I do not know if Herman and the ladies would wish to be burdened with her; in lieu of Gerard?" Matt eyed their guest in query.

The transformation on Herman's face became comical. His perpetual happy grin expanded as his eyes widened. "Why, I am sure the ladies will be more than delighted with a little girl. Jane will be ecstatic, and my Moira will be thrilled to experience caring for a little girl again. She is the eldest in her family and tended her younger sisters when their mother passed away. Besides, she needs the practice; we are starting a family of our own you know!"

Herman proudly shared his news with them.

"Congratulations!" Exclaimed a beaming Matt. "When is it due?"

"Hey! Steady on, we have barely got the wheels oiled. The main reason I enticed you to lend me the children the first time, was to get my missus a little clucky. It worked alarmingly well, thank you, we may end up with three or four; now that we are well housed and settled!"

"Arrgh! I knew you had an ulterior motive, we women can always sense these things. Oh I am so happy for you both. Now don't you go exerting the strength of Moira too much? My word, that is very good news!" Yvonne smiled happily as she poured more tea all round.

CHAPTER TWELVE

The Happy Holiday

Jeremy stood in the doorway of the kitchen with mouth agape. His multiple jobs about the farm having been concluded, the boy had just returned for breakfast, when his mother mentioned that Gerard and his family were going away for the coming school holidays.

"But gee, Mum!" He worried. "I won't have anyone to play with. We were going fishing and maybe camp overnight at our peninsular!"

"Whoa!" Yvonne called. "Who said you could go camping by the river?" Jeremy reddened.

"Arrgh! Me and Gerald were going to ask if we could, it is going to be boring without him;

can't he stay here with us?" Yvonne was very firm.

"No Jeremy, not at all. His Grandma and Grandpa need to have Gerald and Leanne up to their place for awhile and the whole family is going away. You will just have to face facts. You can play with Karen; she needs someone to play with too!"

"Ah gee! She is a girl, she can't go fishing!"

Yvonne had a wicked gleam in her eye as she watched for her son's reaction.

"Maybe not, but Mister Gordon can." Jeremy looked up sharply.

"What do you mean Mum? I know he can fish, he is a really good fisherman!"

The boy frowned at his mother's seemingly off-beat reply. She pouted, and then casually asked.

"If you can't go fishing with Gerard, would you like to fish with Mister Gordon?"

Jeremy visibly brightened.

"Golly, true Mum, how do you know he would let me?"

The boy's gaze centred fixedly upon his mother as he awaited her reply.

"Mister Gordon came to visit your father and me last night!"

"Did he, ah gee Mum, why didn't you wake me?"

"He rang first and waited until you were asleep. He wants to take you away with Missus Gordon – for a week – what do you think of that?"

"Truly? But Gerard can't go!"

"He knows that. We rang Missus Lonard to make sure. Gerard is definitely going away!" Yvonne let that sink in before asking her son again.

"Now, would you like to have a holiday with the Gordon's or not? It is up to you Jeremy, they would really like to have you stay with them but you will have to keep an eye on Karen, when she is in the pool!"

"Gosh is Karen coming too?"

Jeremy's wide brown eyes sought confirmation of this incredible fact.

"Yes Dear. When Mister Gordon found that Gerard could not go, he thought you would need someone to play with rather than be alone. Daddy asked if he would like to take Karen to keep you company. Mister Gordon was delighted to take her along. He thinks Missus Gordon would make a fuss over her!" Jeremy eagerly confirmed this thought.

"I reckon Missus de Lune will make the most fuss, she gave us a great big hug! She likes us to call her Aunt Jane. I think it is great, and she makes great cakes, I think Missus Gordon makes better ones though!"

"I see, so my cakes are not good enough anymore?"

Yvonne impishly teased. Jeremy wrapped his arm about his mother's waist.

"Arrgh gee Mum, Nobody makes better cakes than you do!"

He looked up into her face, so she kissed the boy on his forehead.

"Just as well, or I may not make any more!"

The time leading up to the school holidays seemed to drag for Jeremy. He discussed their situations with his pal Gerard, at school. Gerard bemoaned the fact that he had to go to his grand parent's house, even though he was looking forwards to it.

"I think I would rather go fishing with Mister Gordon too!" He grizzled.

"Yeah! We catch lots of fish with him and we had lots of fun in the pool!" Jeremy recalled.

"Gramps has a pool too, although its not quite as big as Aunt Jane's – it's pretty good but!" Gerard admitted, not wishing to be out-done.

"How long will you be at your Gramp's place?"

Jeremy looked with interest for his playmate's reply.

"At least two weeks – maybe three – Mum says it depends on how Gran and Gramps can cope with us – whatever that means."

Gerard and Jeremy sat cogitating. Then the latter spoke.

"Maybe the last week we can go fishing together. Mister Gordon only wants me for a week."

"What are you going to do when you get back?"

"Don't know, it is going to be boring without you to muck about with!"

Both sat quietly, racking their brains for the answer to their dilemma.

"I'll ring you as soon as I get back!" Gerard promised.

"Hope you only stay two weeks at your Gramp's place!" Jeremy wistfully mumbled. "Don't know what I can do when I come back from the Gordon's if you are not back by then!"

Gerard swished a stick he was toying with in a large circle upon the ground, as he sighed.

"Yeah! Sometimes I think parents should ask what we want, instead of just telling us – but I do want to see Grandpa and Grandma again – they always make a fuss of us!"

The school bell clanged its message calling the children back to their classes.

. . . .

School holidays had begun. Gerard and Leanne were on their way to an exciting couple of weeks with their grandparents. Their parents rejoiced in the fact of two weeks freedom alone, and a blessed relief from the constant drag of farm life. Matt and Yvonne Purcell, although still tending their farm and orchard, were at peace in the calming quiet of a child-free week. Although they would worry a little and miss their children, they were looking forward to the first real break away from the constant care of the children. This would be the nearest thing to a holiday that the happy couple would experience, since the advent of young Jeremy those many years since.

Herman and Moira were motoring along the highway with eager expectation of a wonderful week ahead of them, knowing that the two quiet children strapped in seatbelts on the back seat of Herman's station wagon, would liven up their lives and keep them on their toes.

"I do hope everything goes fine Love!" Herman quietly cooed to his smiling wife.

"Yes Dear, it is bound to be fine, we will be one big happy family. Oh, I am positively bursting with excitement having the youngsters to attend, we are sure to have a wonderful time. I was so thrilled to have the boys for the week-end; but a week – gorgeous!"

Moira squeezed her man's arm.

"Thank you Dear for arranging it, and the little girl – what is her name – oh, I know, Karen; she is such a sweet little thing!"

Quiet settled in the station wagon as it purred along the highway. The children were sitting in sedate politeness, Karen a little apprehensive, but Jeremy agog with the thrill of quality fishing times with his hero. Before long, the children tired of silently watching the scenery and succumbed to the lulling purr of the engine and the gentle vibrations of the roadway; both fell asleep. Herman glanced momentarily over his shoulder to speak to his young guests, but seeing them asleep, cocked his head at Moira for her to witness the children sleeping.

"Oh Herman, aren't they cute, the little dears!"

Herman's station wagon came to a stop outside Jane de Lune's house. The two youngsters slept on as Jane came bubbling out of the front door to greet her guests. Moira put a finger to her lips as Jane approached, insinuating silence; so that Jane could behold the sleeping pair in the back of the vehicle.

"My oh my, isn't the little girl a cutie? Do wake them Hermie – I will help you with the bags – we are going to have a fun week. Gosh, I hope the weather holds good for us!"

As the Gordon's had arranged to pick up the children very early that Saturday, it was just at lunch-time when all arrived at Jane de Lune's home. The children were shown to their rooms and allowed to un-pack their travelling bags. Jeremy was again in the room he had previously shared with his pal, Gerard. Karen was housed in a smaller room next door, where it would be easy for her to seek solace from her older brother, should she be in need of comfort. The scrumptious lunch spread on Aunt Jane's table, soon had the ogling children at ease in their different environment. As expected, Jane had the children one at either side of her so as to better attend their needs and make them feel comfortable and at home. Although at times a precocious youngster, Karen became coy and subdued in this company of strangers. She kept peering past Aunt Jane to assure herself that her brother was still about, and, seeing he was in high spirits, began to loosen up a little. Jane passed a small portion of raspberry jelly with a dob of ice cream upon it, to Jeremy. The ice cream slipped off and fell onto a slice of buttered bread with hundreds and thousands sprinkled upon it, which was set beside Karen. The accident brought forth a merry chuckle from both children.

"Oops, sorry, aren't I a butter-fingers?" Jane excused. "It is nice to hear you so happy. Who would like an ice-cream fairy-bread slice?"

"Oh, me please!" Both children chorused.

"Soon fix that up!" Jane smiled as she put another scoop of ice-cream on Jeremy's fairy-bread slice. The mis-hap broke the slight tension that Karen was feeling and before long, encouraged by Jeremy, who did not feel out of place having already stayed a week-end with Aunt Jane; both youngsters began an easy inter-action with the adults.

"What are we doing today, Mister Gordon?" Jeremy asked, his wide brown eyes glued to his mentor's face, in anticipation of a fishing-type reply.

"After a long ride and a nice lunch, I want you both to have a rest on your beds to let your lunch settle. Sleep if you can, then later, as it is a nice warm day, you may swim in the pool!"

"Oh. I thought we might go fishing!" Jeremy said, a little despondently.

"Now don't you fret young man?" Moira cooed. "We are going camping for a few days starting tomorrow. There will be plenty of time for fishing!"

"Wow! Camping – really?" Jeremy showed his appreciation with a huge bright-eyed smile.

"Me too?" Karen asked.

"Yes dear, all of us. Won't that be fun?" Aunt Jane confirmed.

"May I be excused please? I am going to rest up so I will have lots of energy." Jeremy stated.

"Me too!" Karen echoed. The eager children hurried to their rooms, leaving the adults to talk amongst themselves of the morrow's camping excursion.

The afternoon romp in the swimming pool was an enjoyment for all. As Karen needed to be attended, the ladies sat on the steps in the water and talked. Herman swam with Jeremy and tossed the boy from his shoulders while Karen stayed with Moira and Jane. Soon, the males joined the females at the shallow end of the pool, so Karen and Jeremy could play splashing games together. While enjoying the children's happy frolicking, the caretakers conversed.

After an early attendance at church the next day, Portman's creek was the destination for the campers. The three adults and two children were on their way by nine o'clock. It was a very happy and excited group of people who sang merrily as they motored along. Jane de Lune had been a vaudeville singer in her younger days and still had that beautiful voice of the trained chorus girl. Although unfamiliar with many of the tunes that the adults sang, the children sat in awe of the beautiful melodies to which they were listening, after attempting to follow the repetitive lines in their own style. The adults did encourage the youngsters to sing by falling back occasionally, upon modern songs of the day which they felt the children would know; such as nursery rhymes and jingles. Herman drove off the beaten track once they arrived at their destination. He broke new ground and forged a way into the higher part of the ranges, almost a kilometre from the normal camping areas where fisher folk were likely to gather. He found a little glade well covered from the nippy morning and evening breezes, by a reasonably dense wind-break of shrubbery. Camp was set up and the tents erected. Once the camp was satisfactorily arranged and the li-loes, bedding and tables in place, all sat about the picnic tables for a cuppa, drinks and some lunch. The afternoon was heaven to both children. Jeremy fished with his hero and the quiet of the bush, punctuated only by the merry rippling of the trout stream and the multitude of bird life. The fishing was so good that the pair caught great catches fairly early; then decided that was enough fishing for the time being and headed back the short distance to camp. Karen and the two ladies contented themselves gathering wild orchids and bark of various colours, which Jane would use to teach Karen how to make bark pictures with; at a later time. The evening meal was early so everything could be cleared before nightfall. Fish of course, was the main meal, accompanied by potatoes baked in foil, as were the fish. Julienne carrots, the potatoes garnished with butter, and a squeeze of lemon to taste upon the fish; made the meal quite delectable. The children were to be permitted to stay up for a little while around the campfire when nightfall came, in order for them to experience the flickering eeriness of an evening in the bush, around a camp-fire. But as yet, nightfall was an hour away; both youngsters were allowed a little free time to play.

Karen and Jeremy were tossing a ball to each other as the ladies prepared a bush-type story for them to enjoy around the fire later. Herman was checking his four wheel drive wagon for any equipment which may be needed, and making sure the ice-box was sealed properly, etcetera. His main worry was to be sure the lanterns were ready for use and that the torches were easily available. Karen threw a mis-guided ball over Jeremy's head. It hit a tree behind him and bounced into the oncoming twilight and surrounding bushes.

"Stay there Karen, I will get it!"

The boy called as he went after the ball. He disappeared into the deep shrubbery. Karen patiently awaited his return. Jeremy found the bushes denser than he imagined them to be. He left the faint trail and foraged amongst the grasses where he thought the ball had fallen. A tiger snake hissed a warning, making the boy leap away in fear. He decided to leave the ball where ever it was and go back to the safety of the camp. There was no firelight to guide him and no noise from the camp either. Jeremy realized that he was not sure which way camp was. He called out but there was no answer, so he carefully walked towards camp with an eager eye out for snakes which may be about. Bush bred, Jeremy had no real fear of snakes but was taught by his father to keep a healthy respect of them. Normally he would not get lost, especially so near to camp, but this was strange country to him and he strode with due care in the direction he fancied that camp was situated. He called again, and then heard a faint answering call behind him. Jeremy knew he had been going in the wrong direction.

CHAPTER THIRTEEN

A Frightening ordeal

Karen waited patiently for her brother, as younger sisters tend to have to do. Jeremy seemed to be away for a rather longer period than it would appear necessary. Karen called softly to him for fear that her brother may get into trouble for wandering out of sight. When Jeremy did not immediately return to her soft call, Karen became worried, so she walked over to ask if someone should go and fetch him. Herman was still busy at the vehicle so Karen went to Missus Gordon and Aunt Jane. They were listening to a newscast on the radio; it was not loud but they were engrossed in the news. Hence Jeremy's call passed unnoticed. The boy was not unduly stressed by the fact of going the wrong way. He was more embarrassed at his own stupidity. Jeremy knew the faint answering call must only have come from the camp, so it was natural that in some few minutes he would be back there. Careful of snakes and the odd prickly bush, the youngster manfully strode on; assured that even though the countryside was unfamiliar, he was definitely going in the right direction this time. Calamity struck suddenly and unexpectedly. Jeremy stepped off a mound onto what he thought was solid footing; it was not! Soil covering the rotted timber of a sealed mineshaft, separated with the disintegration of that rotted timber. Jeremy's surprised shriek reverberated within the pit as he fell headlong the five metres depth of the shaft. His shirt brushed an out-poking root which held him long enough to turn his headlong fall, so that he alighted on his feet in an upright position upon the ages of soft dirt that padded the bottom of the pit. The boys' legs crumpled slightly beneath him as he sank into the dirt up to his knees, but the curly black head fell forwards against the hard dirt wall. Jeremy lost consciousness.

Karen's worried face had the two ladies lose interest in the newscast.

"What is the problem dear, won't Jeremy play with you?" Moira asked.

"He chased the ball and he hasn't come back!"

"Oh, I see. I think he must be hiding from you, don't worry Dear, it is just a game."

Jane was looking in the direction of the children's game. She frowned as she stated.

"I do not think it is a good idea to play hidey in this thick shrubbery, he could get lost you know, and there are snakes!" Jane called her brother and explained her fears.

"Good grief no! You are quite right Sis, don't worry, I will go and hunt the little scamp back. You three stay here; we don't want us all to get lost!"

His smile put the three females at ease and off he went, calling to the youngster to come out immediately. Although Herman searched very thoroughly in the immediate vicinity of the camp site, calling as he did so, Jeremy did not respond. Nor was there any sign of the youngster. Herman returned to the ladies with a worried frown.

"Is he back yet?" He asked, hopefully. The ladies replied in the negative.

"Maybe he just wandered a little bit. Stay put, I shall look further out; back in five or ten minutes. Do not worry, I will find him, the little rascal!" Herman set forth again.

A painstaking search a little away from the earlier places, in which he looked, again frustrated Herman. He began to have morbid fears for Jeremy's safety. The river would be the logical place to look for the boy, but as it was on the other side of their camp; it became more obvious that his little guest and ward may indeed have met with an accident. Or perhaps foul play, heaven forbid! If the boy was just lost and wandering, surely he would have answered Herman's repeated calls! The big game warden was not the best tracker in the world but he did have some experience in such matters, due to the nature of his normal occupation. It was with much relief that he did espy a small footprint on a dry patch of dirt where animals had been scratching. It led away from the camp. Herman hurriedly followed in the direction it led. The trail ended in a rocky section and Herman could not pick up the trail again. He used his mobile telephone to enlist help from the local authorities. Herman knew his sister Jane had a portable telephone in her handbag. He rang to ask her to drive to the usual picnic area, a kilometre back down the mountain, so as to lead the coming search party up to their camp site. Herman had already picked up the torch and a snake stick, when he returned to the camp the first time. He continued on, searching alone for the missing boy, whom he imagined would be very frightened by now with the twilight deepening. Herman was berating himself for not keeping a firmer eye upon his young charge and fears for the little body laying alone and possibly injured – or snake-bitten – in this very remote and rough area, had the big man almost in tears. He forged onwards, in the direction he hoped the boy was still going, as he called the lad's name continually. Hope upon hope was that the youngster would stay still and await rescue. Then again, perhaps he may meet the little chap coming back.

"Please God." Herman murmured. "Let him be safe and uninjured!"

Meanwhile, Jeremy began to regain consciousness. It was quite dark and musty-smelling where he was. A faint light filtered down upon the frightened youngster as awareness of his situation came home to him.

"Mum – Daddy!" He called. There was no answer.

Jeremy was cold and his head throbbed. He felt his forehead and discovered a swelling.

"Ouch! That hurts." He mumbled to himself, and then shouted. "Daddy – where are you?" Only the echoes answered. The little boy looked up as if to see them and discovered the opening high above. "Crikey!" He said, in awe. "I must have fallen down a mine!" The realization made him recall where he was.

"Gosh, I've got lost and nobody knows where I am. Mister Gordon will be furious. I don't know what to do!"

The frightened boy let tears run down his grimy cheeks. It was quite dark now and he had no idea that he had been unconscious for over an hour. He tried to reassure himself that his hero, Mister Gordon, would soon find him. In the darkness, Jeremy suddenly realized that he could not move his legs; they felt numb and he found that he could not walk. He panicked.

"I'm paralysed! I must have broken my legs!" He grizzled. "I might die here and no one knows where I am!" He burst forth into pitiful sobbing.

The sobbing dwindled off into snivelling. Jeremy reached down to feel his legs and toes, and then found his fingers on loose dirt up to his knees.

"I'm buried!" He ejaculated in wonder.

The boy found he could easily extract his legs and other than swollen ankles, his legs were fine.

"Phew! Lucky me, jingoes I am freezing!"

Jeremy kept talking to himself the while he flapped his arms about to keep warm, in between healthy cries for help. At times, when he stopped calling out to regain his breath, the silence within his vault of darkness was ominous. Jeremy knew he would die a lonely death of starvation, cold and suffering. He craved mum and dad for comfort, just one last cuddle from them – please God – he would always be a good boy, do his homework and the jobs around the farm, and go to church happily every Sunday. Jeremy fell to the dirty, musty floor; sobbing.

It was a very worried man who stumbled through the darkness of the lonely bush, straining his eyes for the slightest trace of the passing of his little friend.

"The poor little blighter!" Herman kept repeating over and over as he fervently hoped to find something – anything – to give him a clue as to whether he was even going the same way as the youngster had travelled.

"Strewth!" He groaned, as he stumbled on an unseen mound, to go sprawling face downwards upon the ground.

Meanwhile, back at the camp, Moira kept Karen occupied with the making of bark pictures, after explaining that Jeremy must have walked the wrong way but not to worry as Mister Gordon had gone to find him. Jane de Lune flashed the lights of her brother's four-wheel-drive as a small convoy of vehicles approached. She did not stop to address the newcomers but just turned about and led them up to the camp.

As Herman lay face down upon the ground, he found his left hand had fallen into a hole. Gathering the dropped torch, he was about to flash the light from it into the hole, when he stopped to listen. What was that? Faint sobbing. Unmoving he listened quietly. A very frightened, nervous childish voice sobbed pityingly.

"Who – who is there?"

"Jeremy, it is Mister Gordon boy. Are you all right?"

Jeremy burst out crying.

Herman shone his torchlight down and beheld faintly, at the bottom of the shaft, a tearful, dishevelled, shivering and very frightened little bundle.

"It is all right Jeremy. I am here now, everything will be okay. I will have you out in a jiffy – are you hurt or broken Son?"

"My ankles are very sore and my head hurts – I'm sorry – I couldn't help it!" The sobbing continued.

"You have a good cry, I am going to ring for a rope; don't worry, I will get you out!"

In between sobs, Jeremy called.

"I am freezing!"

"Of course, I am a donkey, here Pal, grab my coat and wrap yourself up in it!"

Herman dropped the garment as gently as he could by torchlight, so as not to land it on the shivering child. Another telephone call to his sister had the necessary assistance on the way. Herman continually spoke to Jeremy to calm the terrified boy and reassure him, that help was coming. Jeremy was in awe of the moving patterns of torchlight flickering above him as he heard the many voices of his rescuers approaching. All of a sudden, the pit down which he had fallen was bathed in light, as many torches shone down upon him. Above, a portable flood light stilled the flickering torches, when the area was brightened as of daylight, from the electric generator. Herman's stentorian voice boomed out.

"Back please, get back, we can't afford a cave-in or rubbish falling on the little bloke – move away!"

Jeremy heard a chain-saw buzzing and branches falling. It appeared to be a hive of activity above him. Particles of dirt descended as a solid branch was set across the opening overhead. Jeremy did not know at that time that the branch was part of a winch system, erected to lower one of his rescuers down to his aid. Herman was very keen to descend himself but because of his huge bulk, which would have almost closed the shaft, a smaller chap had the job of securing the cold child into the harness being lowered. As the volunteer adjusted the harness, Jeremy grabbed the man's waist and squeezed, saying very tearfully.

"Thank you – I'm sorry – I'm sorry!"

"There there young Jeremy, it is all in a day's work to me. You should thank Mister Gordon for finding you!"

As the wide eyed tear-stained youngster was winched out of that morbid pit, the outreaching arms of his hero firmly pulled the shivering young lad to safety. He was quickly unbuckled and before he could be placed upon a stretcher for a medical check, Jeremy rushed to cuddle Herman.

"I'm sorry Mister Gordon; I went the wrong way and got lost. I did not mean to, truly!"

The boy squeezed hard, not wanting to let go, perhaps in fear of punishment. Herman softly hugged the little chap when he knelt down to him.

"Jeremy, you are safe now, you won't be punished, I know you did not mean to get lost and I nearly fell into the pit myself."

"Really?"

"Sure Pal, just as well I nearly did or we may never have found you until morning."

Herman eased the boy away.

"Come on Son, be a good lad and lie down on the stretcher; the doctor will need to see how hurt you are. That is a nasty bump on your head!" Jeremy did as his mentor asked.

A balding little man with twinkling eyes who had a very happy smile upon his face, asked where it hurt? A fairly detailed examination was held on the spot and the medico announced that the boy was very lucky that he picked a mine with a soft bottom to fall into. In his opinion there was just the swelling which may turn into a bruise on the boys' forehead. He did not think there was any skeletal damage, possibly sprained ankles which were immediately wrapped in ice packs, but otherwise, the lucky youngster was in good health.

Aside, the doctor advised a little T.L.C. would be in order.

"Do not worry on that score Doctor?" Herman assured. "There are two very anxious ladies at camp who will supply all the Tender Loving Care that this little bloke can handle!"

The happy and successful search party packed up and set forth on the way home, guided by the ample light of the portable power supply. The doctor advised a further check up on the morrow. Herman and another burly man from the rescue squad carried the stretcher upon which Jeremy was rugged up in a thermal blanket, and strapped in for safety; all the way back to the camp site. Herman at the rear handles so as to keep an eagle eye upon his little charge.

CHAPTER FOURTEEN

The Stranger

On advice from the doctor, Herman allowed Jeremy to stay at the camp overnight, as they were assured that the boy only had possible sprains to his ankles and no breakages. If he was not allowed to put weight on his legs, the boy would be better off resting with friends rather than strangers at a starchy hospital. However, Jeremy must be taken to hospital for x-rays the very next day; just as a precaution. Herman would not allow Jeremy to walk anywhere other than for his ablutions. The boy was carried to and from the vehicle whenever travel was necessary, including through the hospital to the x-ray facilities. Upon receiving confirmation that no fractures were present, the boy was advised to rest for a few days at least. The big Game Warden made it his duty to keep carrying the little lad. He would give the boys' ankles every chance to recover quickly. Herman confided to his wife and sister, that he was enjoying the job as nursemaid. Jeremy's days of rest did not adversely affect his holidays. Early mornings found him and Herman at the trout stream fishing, as was their wont. Herman dutifully carried the youngster to and fro, placing the boy comfortably against the bole of a tree where he could easily indulge in his favourite sport of fishing. To fill in other parts of the day, he and his younger sister Karen would stay abed, playing board games. Sometimes, the adults would join them. Karen too, was enjoying her break from the routine of farm life and school. The ladies fussed over the cute little girl, brushing her wavy dark hair regularly and sometimes letting her wear the over-sized slippers of Moira. At such times, Jane would place a garland of flowers upon Karen's head, or perhaps the little girls' ears, with orchids from the bushland. Other interests for both children were Aunt Jane's favourite – bark pictures. These provided a never-ending fantasy as the scrub contained a plethora of the many varieties of coloured barks, which were necessary to pursue this pastime.

The swelling in Jeremy's ankles subsided after two days. He had no adverse effects from his ordeal apart from rather slight bruising to his forehead. Herman deemed the third day opportune for the youngster to walk un-aided. He was firm in his resolve that the lad should not run or jump about for a while. After four days of good fishing, the ladies asked the children if they had had enough of camping. The children were having an enjoyable time at this unfamiliar life-style, and were a little reticent about calling an end to it, but the lure of the beautiful swimming pool and three more days of holidaying at Aunt Jane's; had them agree to leave the trout stream. The other enticement to return home was the thought of a lovely hot shower, rather than the sponging down in the tent from a dish of warm soapy water. Although the weather was warm, bathing in a freezing cold mountain stream, was not a risk that the adults would take with other people's children; under their care.

Herman and Moira sat on the steps of the swimming pool quietly conversing while they watched Jeremy and Karen, as they frolicked at the shallow end of the pool, with a large plastic ball. The children's gleeful chuckles permeated the usually staid and quiet home of Jane de Lune. She smiled contentedly as her eyes beheld the vision of family activity and glee, through her kitchen window. With a laden tray of refreshments, the buxom lady joined her guests at the poolside.

"Hot scones and iced coffee anyone?" Was her welcome call.

The children did not hear as they were enjoying noisy splashing and tossing of the huge ball.

"Scones and lemonade!" Herman's stentorian voice boomed.

"Yippee, great!" Jeremy called. "Come on Karen, scones and lemonade."

The children hurried to join the adults. Both ladies each held a towel with which to dry the happy youngsters; enjoying the experience.

"Did you have a nice swim Dear?" Moira asked of Karen. The wavy black locks sprayed water about as she silently nodded in the affirmative. Once dry enough, the children sat about the out-door table with the adults; enjoying the snack provided.

"That was fun!" Jeremy happily admitted, his bright-eyed face almost hidden behind a very large scone, laden with jam and cream.

"Hello the house!" A strange male voice called, from outside the gate of the high-fenced back yard.

"Who is it?" Jane called back.

"John Sleghorn – could I talk to you for a moment please?"

"The gate is unlocked, come in!" Jane invited.

A dapper little man with a huge brief-case entered. He wore a pin-striped suit and had a rather tight-fitting hat upon his head. The man politely lifted his hat as he approached the group.

"Hope you are not selling insurance." Herman frowned, as he asked.

"Oh no – no – goodness me no. I am a pool accessories salesman. I heard the children splashing in the water so I knew I had the right house. We have a list of homes where people have had their swimming pools serviced by us, and we follow it up by supplying little extras – especially where there are children involved!" His oily smile was not at all encouraging.

"Oh, thank you, but I have enough accessories for my needs thank you!" Jane de Lune advised.

John Sleghorn was a typical salesperson. He pushed his products persistently. Even when told flatly that his services were not needed, still he found another item to push.

"See this photograph of our wonderful floating plastic horse – puncture proof – full of polystyrene and a marvellous toy for such a sweet little lady as this one to enjoy."

The salesman fastened his gaze upon Karen. She quickly looked away.

Herman rose, taking the man by the elbow, he firmly ushered John to the back gate.

"Thank you! You heard the lady; she has no need of your products – good day!"

Herman jostled John Sleghorn through the gate and locked it.

Outside, the salesman "Harrumphed!" Began to walk away, and then stopped. He returned to the gate and peered through the crack afforded by the large hinges. His gaze centred upon Karen, she was giggling at something her brother said.

"Couple of nice little kids." He mumbled to himself. "Now if only I can get them alone, I may be able to con them into asking their parents for some of our products. The boy would love our kick-practice speedboat and I am sure that cute little girl would go for the ride-on seal!" John Sleghorn walked away mumbling to himself.

The very next day was a warm and sunny one. Both children had enjoyed an afternoon swim and were sunning themselves as they sprawled upon towels spread on the lawn, which was nicely trimmed and formed a 'u' shape, around the back and sides of the tiled perimeter of the swimming pool. A lovely garden of annuals grew abundantly between the lawn and the fence. It was a quite narrow garden of about a half metre width. To get the full benefit of the afternoon sun, the children were facing the fence. Jeremy was idly watching a bee as it went about its business. Karen being more interested in the flowers was lightly fondling them.

"You mustn't pick the flowers Karen." Jeremy warned. "Aunt Jane will be cross with us if you do!"

"I am not picking them Jeremy." Karen defended. "I only want to stroke them – they feel nice!"

"Well, you had better watch out for the bees, you might get stung!"

Jeremy's warning was opportune, for an inquisitive bee buzzed over Karen's hand as he spoke.

"Ouch!" Karen jumped away.

"Did he get you?" Jeremy worried.

"No – of course not – I was too quick!"

"Then why did you yell and jump away?"

"I got a fright, that's all!" Karen pouted.

"Pssstt, children!" A voice sounded from the other side of the fence.

"What is that?" Karen asked, her wide brown eyes looked to her older brother for the answer.

"It was someone outside the fence!" Jeremy whispered, and then quietly enquired.

"Who is it?" The answering voice sounded familiar.

"It is I, John Sleghorn."

"What do you want?"

"I need to talk to you without your parents knowing!"

The children remained quiet as they analysed the implication of the stranger's answer.

"We are not allowed to talk to strangers – Dad said!" Jeremy informed.

There was a moment's silence, and then the voice pleaded.

"But I am not a stranger; you met me yesterday at the pool."

"What do you want, why are you talking to us?" Jeremy frowned, with a little annoyance as he asked.

"I would like you to ask your parents to buy you a couple of my swimming pool toys – I have some beauties you know – speedboats you can kick-paddle, and the little girl would love our pretty seal that you can ride on; they are really nice. I have lots and lots of other nice things too, like snorkels and flippers, real skin diver ones they are -!"

Jeremy said.

"I already have a snorkel and flippers, I have goggles too!"

John Sleghorn knew that children were pushovers for sales gimmicks, so he struck with his 'piece de resistance'.

"If you can get your parents to buy the great car and the sweet and cuddly seal, guess what? Each of you will receive free, one of our 'Bubble Blue' beach balls!"

John peered into the crack through which he was speaking, to gauge the reaction of the children to this wonderful bargain.

"I like beach balls." Karen stated, eagerly. Jeremy was more reserved.

"We already have a beach ball, a huge one, anyway; we are not supposed to talk to people we really do not know. Come on Karen, let's go!"

Jeremy jumped up, gathered the towels and dragged Karen away; back to the house.

"Wait!" They heard John Sleghorn call, when they were too far away to be further cajoled.

Herman came out through the back door as his two small guests were running up.

"I have been looking at the pool and you were just not playing in it; where were you?" He asked.

"Just by the fence at the back of the pool, we were sunning ourselves on the towels." Jeremy enlightened.

"Ah! No wonder I could not see you, the lawn dips away to the fence just there. Did you enjoy your day?" Herman put an arm about the shoulders of each of his charges and ushered them inside. "Time to shower and get ready for dinner, children – off you go – hoppit!"

Dinner was always a pleasant experience at Aunt Jane's home. Manners were important, Aunt Jane would stand no bad manners and children were expected to be quiet unless spoken to, however, these rules were not rigidly adhered to. The children were encouraged to politely join into conversations, which they usually did – well – Jeremy usually did; Karen was still a little shy. It was a casual remark by Moira that caused a stilted hush to be noticed by Aunt Jane.

"Wasn't that John what's-his-name a queer little man, you know, that commercial salesperson yesterday. He looked so queer in his pin-striped suit. Oh! And that funny tight little hat!" Moira shook her head in wonderment at the recollection.

"I do not have time for people invading one's privacy with business enterprises!" Herman stated.

"Oh, I don't know" – Moira mused – "sometimes the house-to-house salesperson comes up with very nice items. What about the Vanity Lady who sold me that wonderful make-up kit? I really did enjoy that and you said it made me look gorgeous!"

"But dear, you look gorgeous anyway; you don't need that gimmicky rubbish!"

Herman had a mischievous grin on his face as he attempted to bait his wife.

"Flattery will get you everywhere!" She haughtily answered, belied by the grin which accompanied her reply.

Jane was studious.

"I am on Herman's side regarding salespersons invading one's private domain though, and yes, I did think he looked funny. I hope we do not get bothered by him again." She frowned as she spoke, looking to the children. "You two have gone very quiet – do you have a problem?"

Jeremy blushed and Karen tightly pressed her lips together as she guiltily looked at her plate.

"Hello! What are you two hiding?" Jane coaxed, her eyebrows raised in query.

Herman too, noticed the youngster's embarrassment and tried to put them at ease.

"Don't be afraid to speak up, you could not have done anything really bad. What do you know that we do not?"

Jeremy looked uncomfortable but manfully spoke out.

"It is that man you talked about, John – Mister Sleg-something --!"

"Mister Sleghorn?" Herman interrupted.

"Yes sir! He just spoke to Karen and me through the back fence!"

Moira looked shocked, yet sceptical.

"You mean he came back today?"

"Yes Missus Gordon. He wants us to talk you into buying some things for the pool so we can play on them!" The little lad's face went redder.

"And he promised us a big beach ball – each!"

Karen uncharacteristically blurted her brown eyes wide and alert.

"The devil!" Herman expostulated.

"No – he did not mention a devil!" Karen innocently stated.

The adults tried hard to hide their smiles.

"I think I might just ring that pool cleaning company and have a word to this salesperson. He is a sneaky little twerp!" Herman snapped.

"What is a twerp, Mister Gordon?" Jeremy asked, albeit in ignorant bliss.

"Mister Sleghorn is a twerp Jeremy. Anyone who sneaks in the back door when the front door has been slammed in his face is a twerp!"

"I didn't hear anyone slam a door!" Karen admitted, and then was at a loss to understand why Jeremy giggled and the adults suppressed a smile.

CHAPTER FIFTEEN

The Way Home

With only two days before they were due back home, the children were offered a trip to a shopping mall. It was not only for them to enjoy the wonders of a large city, but also an opportunity for the two country youngsters to purchase a gift for each of their parents. The three adults chipped in to pool a sizeable amount of cash, so that the children would be able to obtain something of quality from which their parents would get lasting value. The thrill of the posh emporiums with a breath-taking array of goods for sale, and the flashing neon lights in a multitude of colours; had the children gape in awe. They were not content with the ride up an escalator, so asked could they ride down, and then up again. Their every wish was happily granted, until at last the energetic pair was settled down at a table in the mall, where the adults enjoyed coffees and the youngsters were feted with milk shakes and some short-bread biscuits. A long discussion was held to determine what the youngsters would like to purchase as presents for their parents. It was up to the adults to make suggestions and the two who knew what may be needed in their home, were left to decide which would be most welcome or the better value to their parents. Eventually, the children came to the conclusion that their mother would enjoy and appreciate a new mix-master-come vitamiser; for the kitchen. Jeremy's eyes almost popped when he was allowed to buy a very good quality trout-fishing rod, for his father.

Karen and Jeremy were standing by the doorway of the sporting goods shop, awaiting the adults. The ladies were contemplating the latest fashions in wet-weather gear, whilst Herman was settling the bill for the fishing rod, and discussing some accessories with the salesperson.

"Why, hello children!" A familiar voice saluted. It was John Sleghorn.

"Oh – er – hi!" Jeremy reddened. Karen hid behind her brother.

"Did you speak to your parents about my little talk with you?" John asked.

"Er – yes Mister Twerp – no – Sleg, er Sleg something?"

"Sleghorn, John Sleghorn. Did you tell your parents you would like them to buy some pool toys?" The pushy man asked eagerly.

"Well – er – sort of, I don't think Mister Gordon wants us to talk to you!" Jeremy struggled to say.

"But you have to ask them --!!"

"No they do not!" Herman appeared suddenly and loomed over the little man. "I will thank you to go away and not bother the children again – or I may get angry – go!"

John Sleghorn hastily made his departure.

Not wanting to strain Jeremy's ankles by too much walking, it was decided by Herman that all should attend a one hour movie showing in the Mall Cinema. This was instigated by young Karen, who noticed some ponies in the advertisement for the film on the bill board outside the theatre. It was a country-style movie that all enjoyed. Jeremy felt strange sitting in the packed theatre with his father's new fishing rod, even though it was packed in a container. Aunt Jane nursed his mother's surprise mixer. Two very tired children were sound asleep after the evening meal was partaken, so they were woken, showered and sent to bed. Aunt Jane had no need to talk them to slumber land with one of her stories. She had lightly kissed each child on the forehead and departed for preparation of the morrow's picnic lunch. It was to be another nice day out at the trout stream and then on home for the children, after lunch.

Herman was standing in the doorway of Jeremy's room, gazing at the sleeping boy. He squeezed Moira a little tighter as he whispered.

"Is he not a wonderful little man Dear? His parents must be so proud of him; I would love to have a youngster like that to call Son!"

"Yes dear, it is a pity we can't keep him. I am beginning to love these little guests of ours. Let us look upon Karen, she is a real cutie!"

The two stole over to the sleeping girl. Her pretty face angelic in sleep.

"Oh Herman, I can't wait to have our own two children, just like these." Moira whispered. "I feel sure we will make wonderful parents. I am looking forwards to our own family!"

Herman embraced Moira and they kissed lovingly.

Portman's creek was as ever, trickling along with the gay abandon typical of mountain streams. Chill water, a haven for the elusive trout, merrily gurgled its melodic notes as the rocky spillways aerated the water. In quiet pools overhung by willows and gums, the quarry of visiting fisher folk went about their silent daily routine. Bush birds trilled or squawked as they flitted about in the terraces of the giant weeds. Being a week-end, there happened to be other folk frequenting this popular fishing area. The females of Herman's group were hard at their chosen hobby of bark picture making, on the blanket spread beside Herman's four wheel drive vehicle. Herman and Jeremy were sitting a few metres apart, each fishing from a quiet backwater. A lovely calm settled upon their quiet corner and Herman glanced at his eager little companion, as the boy let a trout take his cork under. Herman eyed the boy with quiet content as the little lad's face mirrored his enthusiasm in striking gently but firmly; then smoothly reeling his catch in to the net that was awaiting the event, just below the water's surface. The gleam of the happy fisherman shone from the boy's countance as he held the nice trout aloft, for his mentor's approval. Herman nodded his head and pretended to clap. Jeremy re-baited and cast his line again, a contented gleam upon his face. Herman was imbued with pride for his young associate's expertise. Again the big man sighed, as he recalled the happy associations which the meeting of Jeremy and his pal Gerard, had awakened within him. That the boys, and yes indeed, young Karen, had caused Herman to realize just what he was missing having no children; came home to him with a very deep yearning, to become a complete family with his own children. He and Moira must plan for a family and rear them just as fine as these other people's youngsters.

With a very nice bag of trout, both browns and rainbows, Herman and Jeremy packed up their fishing gear and returned to the ladies, for the promised picnic lunch. Moira was preparing the chicken pieces while Jane and Karen packed up the bark picture scraps, having selected a very nice picture that Aunt Jane had made for Jeremy. She assisted Karen in making her own, so that each child also had a present as a memento of their holiday week at Jane de Lune's home.

"Wash up boys!" Moira called with a happy smile. "You know where the basin of hot suds is!"

Missus Gordon's picnic hamper was ever a wonder for Jeremy and he lost no time in telling his little sister Karen, about the wonders that their host usually supplied.

"There are always nice big chicken pieces and frozen jellies – and cakes – Missus Gordon makes great cakes; and lemonade and lollies -!"

"Come on you two, are you going to gossip all day while we eat the goodies?"

Moira called to the children. They quickly sat about the said goodies and their wide open eyes attested to the fact that nothing would be left to waste.

"Well now children, back home to your parents after lunch. Have you both enjoyed your stay with us?" Moira passed over to the children a glass of freshly squeezed orange juice, as she asked.

"Thank you – yes'm Missus Gordon. I sure did. It was great fun, pity Gerard couldn't have come but!" Jeremy answered.

"I did too!" Karen chirped, and then added. "But I will be glad to go home to Mummy!"

"Good girl. Mummy will be glad to know you missed her. Was it nice making the pictures out of bark?" Jane asked.

"Ooh yes! I am going to show Mummy how to make them." Karen fairly beamed her eagerness.

"Mister Gordon. How long will it take us to get back home?" Jeremy asked.

"Just a few hours Jeremy, it is a long trip but there will not be any stops, so if you go to sleep in the car, we should have you back with mum and dad by the time you wake up!"

Moira looked about the setting, and then spoke to Jane.

"Oh Jane – the photo's – we did not take the photo's!"

Jane promptly went to her handbag and found her camera. The children patiently endured the many snapshots that the ladies wanted.

"That is lovely, children, and thank you!" She applauded.

A car could be heard approaching along the track coming down from the higher part of the mountain, where Jeremy got lost and fell into the abandoned mine pit. It was a vehicle that was vaguely familiar to Jeremy. A lady was driving it and two youths leaned out of the windows as the vehicle passed, yelling to Jeremy as they did so.

"Thanks for the yabbies; we pinched some from your dam!"

"Who on earth were they? Moira asked.

"That is Peter and Larry. They were fishing at our dam one day. It was just before you took me and Gerard fishing that time." Jeremy answered.

"I know that car!" Herman frowned. "But there were two men driving it when I confiscated their line nets. That must be the wife and children of one of them. Strange meeting them way up here!"

"Let us not worry about them, we must break camp and pack up or we will be late getting the children back!" Moira suggested.

With all helping, it was only but a few minutes work before the happy travellers were on their way.

Herman and his merry group had barely begun the trip to return their young guests to their own home, when the five came upon that same station wagon in which the two youths were travelling. It apparently slid sideways on a gravel bend and had left the beaten track. The vehicle was firmly lodged in a sandy tract, where repeated inept attempts to extricate it, had only resulted in the wheels sinking ever deeper; to bury the station wagon up to its sump. The lady driver was ineffectually spinning the wheels, as the two youths futilely pushed in an attempt to remove the sad thing from its predicament. Herman stopped his four wheel drive appropriately so as to attach the winch on the front of his vehicle, to the under-carriage of the stricken station wagon. Asking the youths to stand clear, he easily towed the bogged station wagon to solid ground. Meanwhile Jeremy was conversing with Peter and Larry. Herman unhooked his tow-cable and winced it back into its cradle. The lady was most profuse in her appreciation of this stranger's assistance. Herman frowned as he glanced into the holding compartment of the station wagon, only to recognize yet another line-netting arrangement with floats; thrown in the back. Wet bags which he was sure held fish were to be seen.

Mentally Herman recalled the worried look on the lady's face. He surmised that with her man and the other youth's father having been apprehended; no doubt the lady and youths were continuing the poaching. Herman knew it was his duty to arrest them and report this matter, but with his little guests in mind, he deemed it more appropriate to look into the matter another time. It would spoil Jeremy's wonderful holiday were he to arrest the boy's newfound acquaintances' mother right now. Herman would bide his time. The trip back home for Jeremy and his little sister Karen, was uneventful. After a half-hour of sightseeing, both children nodded off and slept peacefully. They awoke to the familiar sound of the vehicle rattling over the cattle-grid at the farm's entrance gate.

"Karen!" Jeremy excitedly called. "We are home, wake up!"

"I am awake silly!" Karen responded, rubbing her eyes. "Quick! Where is Mummy's present?" The little girl twisted in her harness in an attempt to find the treasured gift.

"All in good time Karen!" Herman boomed. "I shall get it for you when we begin to unpack!"

Matt and Yvonne hastily left the house and approached the four wheel drive vehicle as it stopped just by the veranda. Both children gleefully ran to their mother's open arms, excitedly telling of their adventures together.

"Did you have a good time?" Yvonne asked, a question which was already answered by the apparent happiness of the two exuberant youngsters, and their bright smiling faces.

"Mummy, Mummy, I got you a present!" Karen exclaimed, as she was given the mixer, which was appropriately wrapped. The weight was a fraction too much for the little girl, so her brother assisted.

"I have a present for you too, Dad!" Jeremy called over his shoulder. "You won't guess what it is – it's a beaut fishing rod – I picked it out myself Dad!"

All retired to the kitchen where refreshments were prepared. The baggage easily managed by the two men and Jane de Lune. Herman formally introduced his wife and sister.

"So pleased to finally meet you without the rush of departure Moira; young Jeremy speaks very highly of you and 'Aunt Jane'! He had a wonderful weekend at your home the other time and it was not just the swimming pool, he tells me you are both terrific cooks. We must exchange recipes sometime!"

"Oh dear me." Moira answered. "The pleasure was all ours, the children have done wonders for Herman and I; thank you so much for trusting us with them!"

"We were seriously thinking of keeping them, you know!" Jane kidded. "You must lend them to us again sometime!"

Matt and Herman were sitting quietly aside, having their own in-depth conversation.

"So sorry about the mishap Matt, it was stupid of me to relax my vigilance!" Herman apologised.

"Not at all, it turned out all right, no real damage and knowing my young lad; not to be alarmed about. He is an independent youngster and even I could not have prevented it; he is a wanderer!

I must thank you and the ladies for giving us a break from the children; it was good for all of us. Oh, and thanks for the fishing rod and mixer – we should have paid you – not received presents!" Matt reached out a friendly hand. Herman gripped it firmly.

"On the contrary, what your children have done for Moira and I is not to be measured in the colour of gold. They have been a priceless elixir to our marriage and have strengthened our bond in such a way as I could never repay you – or them – I have grown very fond of the children. Thank you Matt, I really do appreciate your faith in us!"

CHAPTER SIXTEEN

An Accident

Jeremy had a quiet week at home helping about the farm and orchard, with his father. Karen enlisted the aid of her mother in trying to make more bark pictures; Yvonne made time and in fact began to find the art an interesting hobby for herself. Upon some occasions, even going so far as to telephone Jane de Lune on the pretext that it was to assist young Karen. A bond of friendship was beginning to develop between them. Upon other occasions it was not beyond the scope of fancy that indeed, Jane rang back to deliver newly remembered advice that she thought may be of benefit. Gerard was still on holidays at his grandparent's house and would be so for the next two weeks, at least. Herman Gordon was now back on the job and he made it his first priority to attempt to catch the lady and the two youths, whom he knew was defying his arrest of their menfolk. He engaged his two assistants in patrolling heavily in the Portman's Creek region. Their task was to seek out the known vehicle engaged in the poaching, and so find the miscreants.

After church on the Sunday of Jeremy's third week off school, Matt decided that a couple of days break would be in order. Whilst the children were away, he had toiled hard and had caught up on those irritating little jobs which were constantly side-stepped. Morning and evening milking was the only really necessary job, as Yvonne and Jeremy normally fed the domestic stock; such as the dogs, chickens etcetera. So Matt announced that the following Monday and Tuesday, he would take Jeremy and Karen fishing. He was very keen to try out his new fishing rod that the children had bought him. Jeremy of course, was ecstatic, Karen a little cautious.

"Won't it be fun dear?" Matt asked of Karen.

She smiled, nodded, and then asked.

"I had enough fishing Daddy. Can't I stay home with Mummy and make more nice pictures?"

Matt raised his eyebrows as he looked to his wife for her reaction.

"You just take Jeremy, Darls; Karen will only hold you up anyway. What say you both gather some nice bark pieces to bring home to us?"

"I will remind you Dad!" Jeremy burst out. "I know what sort Aunt Jane used to get. We'll get heaps!"

Jeremy was very pleased that Karen did not wish to go fishing with them. He liked his little sister and would have encouraged her, but a boy loves to be at one-out with his father; on such occasions.

Nice and early on the Monday morning, the pair set out for a days fishing. All necessary jobs having been attended, the two eager fishermen set forth. Jeremy had extolled the virtues of Herman's secret spot in the area set aside for council use. A telephone call enabled Matt to have permission to fish there, after Jeremy had pleaded with his father to ask. Matt was given explicit instructions regarding the location of the emergency key to the gate. It was cunningly concealed in a cavity behind a numbered post marker. Jeremy implored of his father that he should lock the gate after they had ingress into the property. Matt drove to the shack, checked its security as he did with the explosives shed, then gathering snake-sticks from the lean-to beside the shed; the pair went to the river. A quiet half day yielded three large brown trout each and Matt also caught a medium redfin.

"Gee Dad, you beat me. It must be because of the new rod I bought you!" Jeremy kidded.

"No doubt Son, no doubt. I believe we have enough fish for the present, what say we go put the fish in the ice-box, then go exploring?"

"Gee Dad. What a great idea, come on, I'll race you!"

"Hold on Jeremy – no racing – it is too dangerous!"

"Yes Dad!"

In most directions, the scrub was impenetrable. To the left of the Peninsular was a maze of dead blackberry brambles which had been poisoned; no doubt by Herman and his men. Where they had been fishing was equally thick but only the two trails were there. The normal one where Herman fished and the new trail he blazed with Jeremy, on that occasion when he took the two boys fishing. To the right was also very thick scrub but no blackberries. Evidently they had been cleared from that area upon some other occasion. The scrub was deemed by Matt to be too dense to risk taking his son, due to the threat of snakes.

"We will have to circle around the shack Son and see if the way is clearer closer to the road. It may be possible to get to the river from the right."

He led the way, Jeremy close behind wielding the snake-stick in readiness, as Herman had taught him. A game trail wove in and about the trees and shrubbery. They followed it and the trail led to the river.

The river was not suited to fishing at that spot as it was full of snags and fallen trees. No tree was completely across the river, so there was no incentive to attempt a crossing, even though a huge basin which may well have been good for fishing, could be seen further upstream on the other side of the river.

"Hey Dad!" Jeremy cried out. "Here are two of the paper-bark eucalypts that Aunt Jane uses for her bark painting pictures. Can we gather some for Karen and Mummy?"

"Of course, Son!"

The pair spent ten minutes or so collecting the variety of bark strips and pieces, which would be most appreciated by their womenfolk.

"I'll get some of these dark little bits from that there wattle, too Dad!" Jeremy did so.

As the pair left all their fishing tackle locked in Matt's utility, the happy gatherers were left with nothing in which to carry the bark. Matt solved their dilemma by stripping a large piece of bark off a fallen tree that had begun to warp in the summer sun. A few deft slashes with his pocket knife soon had a viable scooped container, adequate for their needs.

"Right that is more than enough for the ladies Jeremy. We will leave them here and pick them up on the way back. Come boy, let us continue our exploration and see if we can get to that back-water up ahead; it should be unspoiled and I think tomorrow, we may get the biggest trout you have ever seen out of it!"

"Gosh Dad, I hope we can find a way to get to it!" Jeremy enthused.

They forged onwards, through the semi-dense scrub, Matt keeping an eagle eye out for those wriggly denizens of the bush that may strike unseen. When the two explorers eventually arrived at a spot approximately opposite to the back-water in question, both realized that fishing from where they were, would be untenable. Many of the tall eucalypts leaned crazily due to the bend in the river. The flood waters were cutting into the banks, undermining the root systems of many of the trees. In fact, the couple that had already fallen on their side of the river were causing snags that prevented fishing from that side. Matt looked further upstream where he fancied there was a tree leaning halfway across the river. A broken branch hung limply where another tree had broken the branch and left it dangling precariously.

"Stand aside Jeremy!" His father ordered. "I will see if I can push this large tree over. If it will fall, then perhaps we will be able to cross on it, then we can use the back-water to fish from!"

Jeremy stood well back out of harm's way as his father pushed and strained against the large tree. Most of the root system of the tree was lying bare over the river, as the water had really washed the bank away.

"It is going!" Matt gasped to his son. "I had better get a log to push it with or I may fall into the river when the tree falls. There is a suitable branch by that bush Jeremy; grab it for me will you please?"

Jeremy passed the heavy branch to his father. Matt trimmed it by breaking away any small twigs that might impede his wielding it as a battering-ram, and then stood atop the fallen log for better leverage. Much more straining and eventually the weakened root system gave way under the constant pressure. The large tree, already well off balance, began to topple over the river; its huge weight ripping the weakened roots with much tearing of those roots. Of a sudden, the tree succumbed and fell across the water to the far bank with a leafy thud. The dangling branch broke free and bounced off the trunk towards Matt. He tried to leap aside but slipped on the mossy surface of the log upon which he was standing, to fall to the ground parallel to the log. The bouncing branch landed with a heavy thud where Matt had been but a moment since, then slid off to trap the man between the two. As Matt disappeared beneath the leafy mass, Jeremy screamed in horror; fearing that his father was squashed beyond help.

"Daddy – Dad!" He cried in terror. "Oh Daddy – please Daddy – are you all right?"

Jeremy pushed in amongst the leaves, trying to find his father.

"It is all right Son, don't panic, I am not hurt. Can you roll the branch away? Try Son, I will help!"

Both struggled frantically to move the branch but it was beyond the small muscles of the frantic little boy.

"Okay Jeremy, just stop a minute and listen; are you listening?"

"Yes Daddy!" Jeremy began to snivel. "Now don't cry Son, you have to be brave. I am just jammed in between these logs and my arms are pinned so I can't get to the car keys. It is up to you Son, to get help for dad – you can do it – so do not panic and just do as I ask!"

"Yes Daddy." A calmer Jeremy answered. "What should I do?"

"Take the snake-stick and go to the 'Ute. Go slowly and be very careful of snakes, think you can find your way back to the car Son?"

"Yes Daddy!"

"Alright, now you know where the spare tyre is kept under the tray; well just feel under the number-plate area and you will find a little magnetic tin. It is stuck on a ledge just in front of the spare. It has an emergency set of keys in it, I want you to open the car and get the 'phone. Ring Mister Gordon, you will find his number in a diary in the glove box!"

"I have his number on my fishing creel, Dad!"

"Okay – use that – I just have to hope he is not too far away. Go now, and please be careful Son. Wait in the car until he comes or sends someone else. And do not worry, I will be all right!"

"Yes Dad, I'll go now!"

As Jeremy began to leave, his father called.

"Take your time and be careful!"

Jeremy hurried away, snake-stick ready and watery eyes alert.

The worried boy retraced his steps along the way he remembered where his father forged a path through the bush. Being bush bred, he had a good awareness of such things. That he had got lost up in the hilly country of Portman's Creek, was quite understandable in that it was dusk at the time. Jeremy would not get lost this time. Golly, didn't his father's very life depend upon Jeremy finding the way back to their utility and organising assistance? The boy carefully negotiated his way, keeping a very keen eye out for pit-falls, such as an awkward meeting with a snake, or heaven forbid; another mine shaft. Jeremy did not believe there were any old mine shafts on this thickly shrubbed peninsular. His father had told Gerard's father upon one occasion that their farms were not in a gold mining area. Jeremy did not fear another fall into a horrid pit! All at once the little clearing where they had left their vehicle, came into view. Jeremy breathed a thankful sigh of relief as he beheld the utility; parked where it was left. He searched where his father had told him the spare key was located but seek as he would, no little box holding a spare key could be found. Jeremy even went so far as to lay prone upon his back underneath the vehicle to see if he could locate the elusive little box. No, the box definitely was not there! The boy began to panic, knowing that his father could die of thirst or starvation, trapped beneath those heavy logs and Jeremy, his only salvation, could not find the key to save him. The whimpering lad knew he would have to find something to smash a window with, so that he could get to that life-saving telephone. In frustration, he searched about for a stone or some heavy object that would gain him entry to the utility. His search was successful and as he made his way back to the car, ready to force his way in; he distinctly heard a motor approaching. The boy stood still, awaiting it. The vehicle proved to be Herman's four wheel drive. Herman hailed the boy with only slight surprise.

"Ah! Young Jeremy, I was hoping you would still be here. How come your dad is not with you? It is too dangerous for you to be running about alone on this particular peninsular!" Jeremy dropped the rock he had found and ran to his friend and mentor.

"I was just going to ring you, Mister Gordon. I need help. My dad is trapped under a couple of trees!"

"Where Son. Is he hurt? Take me there quickly, no wait a minute, I will get some equipment!"

Herman took Jeremy to the explosives shed where he obtained a chain saw and a crow bar. He also took a small first-aid kit, which he asked the boy to carry.

"Can you find your way back to your father Pal?"

"Yes Mister Gordon, can we hurry please?"

"Let us not break our own necks; we won't be any help to your father then. Did you talk to your father, how is he trapped?"

"Under a big log and another big branch fell on him. He said he is not hurt but his arms are trapped. He could not get his keys out and I couldn't find the spare keys. Gosh I was worried. Then you came; gee, I was glad to see you!"

The two rescuers eventually arrived at the accident site. Herman called.

"How are you Matt – where are you?"

"Here!" Came feebly from the depths of the two large lengths of timber and foliage.

"Anything broken? I will have you free in a minute!"

Herman found Matt and checked the situation.

"I won't try to lift the branch, it may be too heavy and I won't risk it dropping. Hold on until I saw off the ends; then I should be able to release you easily!"

The chain-saw buzzed into action and in less than three minutes, Herman had freed the boy's trapped father. Herman assisted Matt into a sitting position on the mossy log. Matt's arms were numb due to repressed circulation and his right leg was similarly affected. The ankle of his right leg was very bruised and swollen, in fact he asked Herman to remove the boot and so relieve the pain.

"That ankle could be fractured; I think I had better strap it up!" Herman said, and did so. He also cut two saplings and fashioned make-shift crutches.

"Best to keep the weight off that leg Matt!" He advised.

On the way back to their vehicles, Jeremy had the presence of mind to collect the bark pieces that he and his father had gathered. He placed the first-aid kit upon the bark sleeve so as to be able to use both hands to carry the load properly. For the child, it was quite heavy. Herman drove both Jeremy and his father back home in his four-wheel-drive. Once Matt was settled back home in comfort, Yvonne could be driven back to the council property to retrieve their utility. It would be quite safe, locked in the enclosed and restricted area.

"Jeremy, you will have to do my share of the jobs about the farm now Son. Just for a little while, do you mind Pal?" Matt squeezed his Son's shoulder. "You will have to be the man of the farm for a few days!"

"Yes Dad. I can do it!"

CHAPTER SEVENTEEN

Herman Steps In

Herman rang his foreman Pat, to tell him that an emergency had arisen and not to expect his boss back that day. The Game Warden offered Matt and Yvonne his services for the rest of the day. Although both demurred, Herman would not think of leaving the stricken man, when he knew he could be of valuable assistance. Herman drove Jeremy and his father into town so that the damaged ankle could be assessed. The ankle did prove to be fractured and was therefore encased in plaster. Matt was told not to walk on it for at least two weeks. The plaster would remain in place for six weeks. Matt worried for his farm responsibilities. Upon confirmation of the break, Herman rang his employers to request at least two days compassionate leave. This was granted and even though Matt and Yvonne protested; Herman insisted that it was a pleasure for him to help his new-found friends. Jeremy, of course, was thrilled to pieces having his mentor stay for a couple of days. Once Matt was settled at home with his family fussing over him, Herman suggested that Yvonne and he go and fetch the utility back home. Jeremy was made to stay and look to his father's needs. Reluctantly, the boy agreed. Jeremy argued that he could stay with his father anytime but only now and again, could he be with Mister Gordon. The boy brightened when told that he could help Herman with the milking and doing some of the odd jobs that normally fell to his father; after the utility was brought back to the farm. Herman rang his wife Moira. Once she was made aware of the situation, her blessing was granted for Herman to stay for so long as was needed. Yvonne made ready the guest room for her most welcome guest. The rest of the daylight hours found Jeremy shadowing Herman as the two went about the everyday business of running the farm and orchard. Jeremy proudly introduced his hero to 'Bessie'.

"I got her for my tenth birthday and I have only had her for half a year. But I love her to bits, she is easy to ride and she can really gallop when I want her to!"

His pride was mirrored in his face.

The following morning had Gerard's parents ringing to hear how Mat was getting along and to offer their assistance. Matt explained that he could not expect them to leave their vineyards as they were just as busy as he was. Anyway, Yvonne could manage the seasonal pickers and Herman was attending the stock. What Matt did not explain, was the fact that Herman was only temporarily on hand; for a few days. Percy and Grace Lonard offered their sympathy with a firm promise from Matt and Yvonne, to call upon them for any assistance they may need. Gerard arrived about mid-morning with fishing tackle and a cut lunch. Upon seeing Herman Gordon sipping tea on the back veranda and talking with Jeremy, Gerard gasped.

"So Mum was not kidding, Mister Gordon is really here. How are you Mister Gordon?"

The boy placed his bicycle against the newel of the steps, took the creel off his back and hurried to sit with the other occupants of the verandah.

"I am well Gerard, thank you." Herman replied, then. "Ah! I see you two have made arrangements to go fishing?"

Gerard nodded.

"Yes! Dad and Mum got back from their holidays early and Gramps was getting tired of having us kids to look after; so we came back early too! I wanted to come back and go fishing with Jeremy, anyway!"

"Gosh Gerard, I am glad you're back. It's a pity you can't come with Dad and me, he has a broken foot!" Jeremy sighed. "Dad was going to take me to the beaut new back-water we found. Now he can't, gee, it's not fair 'cause I was looking forwards to fishing there with Dad!"

"Mum said a tree fell on him and he could have died!" Gerard whispered in awe.

"He got jammed between a log – a huge log – and a whopping big branch that fell on him!" Jeremy enlightened his cobber.

"Gee! He must be the luckiest dad alive!" Gerard gasped.

"Yeah!"

Herman excused himself from the company of the two boys, mentioning that he had better take the cup inside so that it could be washed. He went into Matt's room where the invalid was fretting.

"You don't look too happy Matt." Herman sympathised. "Ankle paining?"

Matt shook his head.

"No, the ankle is fine. I am so frustrated being stuck here and leaving Yvonne to manage things. Crikey! The house, kids, washing and cooking is too much for her now without having me and the orchard to manage. The sheep will have to wait for tagging now and I am worried about getting fifty to the market!"

"Is there any local help available?" Herman asked.

"Not that I would care to trust. I usually have Percy Lonard – young Gerard's dad – to help, and then I get over to help him with his market-garden. I do have itinerant pickers, whom I may be able to talk into getting off the apples to do a spot of tagging, but I doubt that any would be eager to change jobs!" Matt thought quietly for a moment, and then added. "I don't think any of them would be experienced with sheep anyway. Most of my pickers are city kids working to pay school or college fees!"

"I would love to assist you Matt, but I just took a week's leave to have the children stay with us. I worked on a farm or two up in New South Wales before I got this cushy job with The Fisheries and Game Department. I am experienced with sheep and cattle!"

"No – I would not dare get you into trouble with your employers, you have been quite magnificent as it is and I am much obliged to you – thanks!"

Matt reached out a friendly hand and Herman warmly shook it.

"Oh! Do you have anything pressing for me to do before the afternoon milking?" Herman asked.

"No, I think that is all that is left for today. Yvonne and Jeremy can manage the milking if you have to leave --!"

Herman smiled.

"No – no that is not the reason I asked. The boys are disappointed that you are unable to take the two of them to that new spot you and Jeremy found. Jeremy was so looking forwards to having that second day with you." Matt frowned.

"It is bad luck because I was disappointed too. I do not get many opportunities to take my son fishing!"

"Would it worry you if I took the boys for a couple of hours? It may brighten them up. Jeremy is fretting over your injury, you know." Herman raised an eyebrow in query.

"Ah, that is what you were on about. You would do that for me. Gosh Herman, how can I ever repay you?" Matt shook his head in wonder, and then his face brightened. "I am sure the boys will love it and Yvonne will be helped to have the lads out of her hair for a few hours!"

Matt granted his new friend permission to entertain the glum children.

Two ecstatic ten-year-olds eagerly placed fishing tackle into Herman's four wheel drive, then climbed inside the vehicle, chatting happily. Herman acquired a little snack and drinks from Yvonne, prior to setting out on the short trip.

"I can show you the bridge we made. Dad pushed this huge big gum down because it was going to fall soon anyhow, and we made a bridge to cross the river. Gee! I tell you, this is a terrific place to fish from – bet we get some whoppers!"

Jeremy's excitement caused a merry twinkle in Herman's eyes as he was privy to the boy's eagerness.

"Remember boys, when we are close to the fishing area, let us be quiet. We will have a better chance to catch some really nice trout if we do not frighten them into hiding. Remember to grab a snake-stick each. You do remember your instructions regarding snakes?"

Herman quickly glanced at his young companions for verification.

"Yes Mister Gordon!" They answered in unison.

Herman checked thoroughly that the fallen tree which Matt had felled to form a bridge was indeed safe enough to cross. He crossed the bridge twice, and then made sure that the opposite bank was free of pitfalls, such as holes, snakes etcetera; so that his little charges would be safe fishing from the newly-found back-water. Both youngsters were agog with anticipation as they settled quietly to their fishing. The two hours of fishing proved most successful, as the fishing usually was when the boys were in the company of their hero and mentor, Herman Gordon. He was becoming so attached to these two polite and cheery youngsters that he knew he would be at odds with himself when his own child or children were growing up. The big man heaved a contented sigh as he landed another nice trout. The happy faces of Jeremy and Gerard beamed back at him, as they witnessed his good fishing.

When each had caught three nice-sized trout, Herman asked the boys to reel in and wash up for a snack. He led the boys back over the new bridge to the small clearing where Jeremy's father became injured; when trapped under the branch. A small fire was lit and Herman set his camp billy on green sticks above the embers, with cold water from the small river to make hot drinks for all. Three cups of chocolate from the refreshment haversack would suffice to make the few sandwiches prepared, go down more comfortably. Herman sat upon the mossy log with a lad either side of him. The boys had followed his example and placed a piece of dry bark on the log, upon which to sit, so that the moss would not chill them.

"Well now!" Herman exclaimed. "Was that a good place to fish or not?"

Jeremy mumbled with a mouthful of sandwich.

"I'll shay!"

Gerard nodded, too engrossed in his refreshment to speak. When Jeremy had cleared his mouth of food, he was more elaborate.

"I am very glad you saved us from Joey and that Lance, Mister Gordon. Gee we have had some good fishing since you have been our friend; thank you!"

Herman looked with surprise at the boy when he heard this wonderful note of appreciation.

"Why, that is nice of you to say, young man. I have had a lot of enjoyment from having you two as friends too, you know. Sometimes I feel you belong to me and I am getting to love you both as I would my very own children!"

Herman looked at Gerard to see his reaction. The boy agreed with Jeremy.

"If I didn't have a father, I would like you to be my father!" He shyly said.

Herman sensed Jeremy get down from his perch and sidle near. He turned to the boy just as Jeremy wrapped his arms about the huge man's waist and squeezed in a fierce hug.

"I reckon you would be a great father too – I – I love you nearly as much as I do my Dad!" Not to be outdone, Gerard also gave Herman a squeeze.

"Come lads; let us not get too mushy. We are all great friends and you both have wonderful fathers – and mothers. We had better put out the fire, clean up this area, and then get back in time for the milking." This was soon done and the fishing party began the journey back home.

The merry fishermen were welcomed home with their very good bags. Matt thrilled to the ecstasy emanating from his happy son, as the boy re-enacted the day's fishing.

"The bridge we built works great Dad!" The boy enthused. "It is as solid as a rock and it is easy to cross over. Mister Gordon is pleased that it is there because he needed a secret crossing, to catch people who do not obey the fishing laws. He reckons he can come from a new direction now and they won't be expecting him!"

Gerard had ridden his bicycle homewards and Herman had begun milking; when Jeremy suddenly recalled he was obliged to do his own jobs and assist Mister Gordon.

"Oops! I better scoot Dad; I have to help Mister Gordon!"

The youngster rushed off to tend to his responsibilities. Matt cheerily waved his son off, and then frowned at his own stupidity, causing him to be laid up and relying upon others to do the work. He stared fixedly at the wall for a few moments, trying to solve the dilemma of obtaining assistance for a couple of weeks. He came up with a blank and his worried frown increased. From afar, the happy chuckles of his son came clearly to him. A contented smile replaced the frown.

"My word, it is nice to see a smile, you have been very glum lately."

It was Yvonne, who breezed into the room, trailed by Karen.

"Daddy, Daddy, and look I made another picture with the new bark. It is a chook house with lots of chooks in it!"

She leaned against her father's bed while he studied the jumbled maze of bark pieces.

"My goodness, you do have lots of chooks in it. That is a very nice picture dear!"

Matt kissed his daughter upon the forehead. She merrily skipped away to add it to her collection. Yvonne asked.

"What are you smiling about? A broken foot is not funny at this time of the apple-picking season!"

Matt clasped his wife's hand and gently eased her to him. He lightly kissed her.

"I heard that little imp of ours chuckling out there with Herman. At least the children are happy. Gee, the man has been a God-send so far as Jeremy is concerned; the boy seems to have attached himself to the man!" Yvonne suspected a note of jealousy in his tone.

"Ah! Don't go fooling yourself, it is just hero-worship. Since Herman saved the boys from those larrikins and takes the boys fishing; it will do the boys good to have another interest!"

"Yes Dear, I guess you are right. Any ideas about getting some help with the sheep? I hate having to pull Percy away; he has his own labour problems!"

Yvonne had also been in a quandary regarding her husband's inability to cope with the sheep.

"Perhaps the local paper or what about a notice in the window of Jenkins's Store?"

Her widened eyes looked hopefully to her man, hoping the suggestions would brighten him up a little.

"It is a good possibility and there may be a few of the locals interested. Worth a try, I suppose!" He squeezed her hand. "Pity Herman could not stay on for two weeks. Once I am on the crutches I can work the dogs, as I fear Herman would not be able to manage them. Most working dogs obey only the one master; Herman could be so helpful in other ways though!"

"Something will crop up Love!" Yvonne tried to brighten him. "Fresh cuppa, Dear?"

"Ta yes that would be nice."

Herman came breezing into the kitchen with young Jeremy in tow.

"Hello! Where is everybody?" He boomed.

"In the bedroom, Herman!" Yvonne called.

The big man poked his head in through the open door.

"The separating is finished and all the chores completed, so I must be off home; Moira will be awaiting me!"

"Thanks Herman, I owe you one. Have a safe trip and don't forget the box of apples and the meat in the 'fridge!"

"Oh, I will get that!" Yvonne rushed past to get the donations.

Yvonne and Jeremy waved goodbye from the verandah as Herman headed home. A happy grin on the boy's face belied the sadness of losing his mentor, albeit only for the time being. As the tail lights of Herman's four wheel drive vanished behind the trees that abounded along the roadsides; Jeremy withdrew into the house.

"I am going to miss Mister Gordon, Dad." He dismally stated.

Matt ruffled his son's black curly locks. "Ah, don't worry Son; there will be other times for you to be with Mister Gordon. He likes you a lot, you know!" Jeremy brightened.

"Do you really think so Dad?" "I am positive. He told me so himself." The boy hugged his father. "I love you Daddy!"

The telephone sounded. Yvonne answered the call and after a short conversation, entered the bedroom.

"It was a friend of Herman, Dear. He asked if you can spare him a month of work, he is coming to be interviewed tomorrow!"

CHAPTER EIGHTEEN

The New Hand

At seven-thirty the next morning, Jeremy had just finished the milking and had separated the cream from it. As he struggled with the buckets into the cool-room, a smart two-tone station wagon drove over the cattle-grid and came to a stop in front of the house.

"Hello the house!" The driver cheerily called.

It was Yvonne who came to the door in response to the visitor's hail.

"Good morning, Missus Purcell, is it? Herman Gordon said you have a few weeks work available to an experienced farm hand. I rang last night to say I would come for an interview. I am Pat Searle!"

"Oh, yes Mister Searle, we have been expecting you. Would you come in please, my husband is laid up?"

Matt rose to greet the man Herman had recommended his weight dependent on a crutch.

"I believe you are experienced with sheep Mister Searle; is your expertise in that area local?" Matt asked.

"No, and to be honest, it is about five years since I have worked any. I managed to acquire a Government Position and am on holidays. I need the extra work to help pay off my mortgage. I used to muster up in New South Wales on Barnes's run!" Pat explained.

"Mister Searle, I am grasping at straws currently and anyone who has even eaten lamb is most welcome since I stupidly cracked my ankle. If you are able to start immediately, I shall have my wife Yvonne, drive you around the property to familiarise yourself with it; and then I can more easily express my directions to you!"

Matt called Yvonne in and gave her the gist of what he required of his newly hired hand. As his mother and the new hand drove away, Jeremy stood perplexingly looking after the utility. The boy went in to his father.

"Are you going to hire that man Dad?" He asked.

"Yes Son, I really need a strong healthy assistant right now, as I have to get the lambs marked and a shipment mustered; to help pay the fruit pickers. The cannery cheque will not be in until the end of the month."

Matt had a cheery smile on his face, which did not go unnoticed by his son.

"It is nice to see you happy Dad. You have been a bit grumpy since you got squashed. Is your foot really sore?" Jeremy had concern in his eyes as he asked the question.

"No, it is not too bad Jeremy; just a little niggardly ache now and again is all."

Matt sat down on the bed and hugged the boy to him. Jeremy turned to his father.

"Dad!"

"Yes Pal?"

"That man – how did he know that you needed him?" Jeremy stared fixedly at his father; expectantly.

"Oh. I believe Mister Gordon recommended him Jeremy. Why do you ask?"

It was Matt's turn to watch the boy closely.

"I think I have seen him before Daddy, but I don't know where!"

Matt considered this, then off-handed queried.

"Maybe you just noticed him in town or even at the fairgrounds that time you went with Mister and Missus Gordon and Aunt Jane?"

Jeremy pouted as he slowly shook his head, his curls vibrating as of a cascade.

"Don't think so Daddy!"

Pat Searle proved to be most beneficial to the Purcell Family. He did the work required of him well and efficiently. No job was too hard or too trivial for him. His was not a live-in job as was the case with many farm hands. Pat drove off each afternoon after milking and was always at work on time early in the morning; for the dawn milking. He drained the pig-pen, fixed any weak fencing that may have needed attention and was a top hand at tagging, with Yvonne driving Matt out to the fields, so that he could use his dogs for the round-up. The orchard was prospering and after a heavy crop of grass-hay had been harvested and baled for the winter feed; Matt sighed contentedly. His pickers had almost finished the final section of the orchard. Perhaps the last seven days of the month would see the crop out; then would come the pruning and preparation or the next year's yield. It was just before the week-end that would signal the end of the school holiday period and halfway through the second week that the new man Pat had been working; when Jeremy remembered where he had previously seen the man. The boy raced excitedly in to relate the recall to his father.

"Daddy, Dad!" He urgently cried. "Mister Searle, I remember where I saw him before – it was in the bushes!"

"Eh?" Matt worried. "What bushes, what do you mean you met Mister Searle in the bushes?" Jeremy shook his curly head vigorously.

"No, I did not meet him in the bushes, I saw him in the bushes. He was with another man. Do you remember the day we met Mister Gordon and he told us to fish somewhere else – the day he caught the net-fish poachers?"

Matt nodded.

"Yes Son. Go on!"

"Well," Jeremy continued "Gerard and I found two men hiding in the bushes – Mister Searle was one of them. He is a Game Warden too; Mister Gordon told us they were his men. That is where I have seen Mister Searle before!"

Jeremy was wide-eyed as he sought his father's reaction.

Matt nodded his head, thinking. He calmly smiled at his son. "Do you know what Jeremy? That Mister Gordon of yours has actually got one of his men to help out because I was desperate, and I think you may have been a prime mover in activating him too!"

"Yes Daddy. What is a 'prime mover'?" The lad enquired innocently.

Matt ruffled the boy's hair lightly.

"It does not matter. Just remember that Mister Gordon is a wonderful friend of ours and I am most pleased that he took a fancy to you, as a fishing partner. He has been very good to us, so you be on your best behaviour for him, won't you?" "Yes Dad!"

That evening, Herman Gordon rang the Purcell household.

"Yes Mister Gordon, how may I help you?" Yvonne asked, as she answered the call.

"Well, for a start, I believe we are friends enough to be on a first name basis; do you agree?" He asked, hopefully.

"Why of course – Herman – is it not? Please call me Yvonne. Do you want Matt or Jeremy, Herman?"

"Thank you Yvonne – no – as a matter of fact it was you I wished to speak with. Do you have a minute?"

"Oh dear! Of course I do, has it to do with our boy at all?"

Yvonne was intrigued, for at first realizing that it was the Game Warden, she expected the call would have been work-related; to do with the man he had sent.

"Well yes, as a matter of fact it is to do with your young man. I – er – I wish to borrow him, if I may?"

Yvonne was non-plussed, she did not reply immediately as she strove to understand the gist of Herman's proposal.

"Borrow him – borrow our boy – what do you mean Herman?" Herman laughed.

"Oh crikey! That did not come out too well, did it? At the end of this month, that is, the first Saturday of the new month; my employers hold a family day. Barbeque, picnic type affair. They have father and son races and mother and daughter cooking contests, that sort of thing. My family is not due for another eight months, so I have the temerity and gall to ask if I may borrow yours for a day; Karen too!"

Yvonne laughed at him.

"Oh Herman, you can be so rewarding at times. Of course the children would love to spend a day with you; I can imagine trying to hold young Jeremy back. I shall have to check with Matt first though, he may have other plans. I do not think the children would want to miss out on a picnic day – thank you – may I ring you back later for confirmation?"

"Ta, I will be in for the rest of the evening!" Herman hung up the receiver.

Yvonne and Matt discussed the matter about which Herman had telephoned. The two children, Jeremy and Karen, were asked if they would enjoy having another day out with Mister and Missus Gordon. Of course Jeremy jumped at the offer but asked if his best pal Gerard was invited too.

"I did not ask Dear." Yvonne raised her eyebrows. "Perhaps he may think just you and Karen are enough trouble for him!"

"Aw! Don't make jokes Mummy, this is serious!" Jeremy cocked his head to one side as he gave what he thought was a severe look. "Can I ask him if Gerard can go too, please?" Yvonne kissed her son on the nose, and then offered.

"Your father is to ring Mister Gordon in a few minutes; perhaps you had better leave it to him!" Jeremy hurried to his father.

"Hello Missus Gordon. Matt Purcell here, that bounder of yours asked if he could borrow my children!"

"My word yes, he told me you must have thought he was dealing in stock. I am sorry if he seemed a little crude but --!"

Matt cut in.

"Not at all, I know he has a heart of gold and his intentions are good. The children are eager to have a day out with you and I would deem it an honour for you to have them for the day. Especially after that very kind and helpful deed he did for us!"

"Oh I am so happy, thank you. I do so love having the little ones here. Er – you have me puzzled – of what kind and helpful deed are you speaking?" Moira seemed genuinely intrigued.

"Do you mean you did not know about Pat Searle coming to work for me?"

"Why, no – I had no idea – I thought Pat was still on the job with Herman. Do you mean to tell me that Herman has fired him?"

Matt was quiet for a moment, and then replied.

"I am not sure about that, but when Pat came looking for work; at that time I did not know he had been in employment with Herman. I believed he was catching some extra time for a house payment or something. Mind you, I am very happy with his work, he seems to be bending over backwards to be as helpful as he can be. I was hoping Herman would enlighten me!"

"Hold the line Mister Purcell; I shall fetch him that is the only way to sort things out!"

Moira said. Matt heard her calling her husband to the telephone.

"Hello Matt! Am I to be a family man for the day?" Herman boomed over the wire.

"There is no trouble there. The children are eager to go and I think that it is common sense to be on a first name basis, Herman. Yvonne explained your call. Just one thing though!"

"Yes Matt. Is it as serious as it sounds?" Herman queried.

"What is going on with your man Pat, has he been dismissed?" Matt held on expectantly.

"Ah! Did he say something?"

"No, not at all; it was young Jeremy. He recognised Pat from the day when you sent the boys away to fish somewhere else!"

Herman explained that as Pat was due holidays but wished to work on, as he had financial problems, he was asked by Herman to take his holidays from the Fisheries Department and earn the extra money by helping at the farm. This allowed Pat to have a double income for the period which was a financial boon for him, and let Herman off the hook – so to speak – as he had already taken his time off; well, part of it anyway.

"Thanks for organizing that Herman, you do not realize what a boon you have been to us!" Matt applauded.

"It was the least I could do for you Matt. You and your family have been so good to me and mine, that I felt I would never be able to repay you. At least now I feel that I have contributed something back to you!"

"That is a two-way street – incidentally – I know you told me you worked on a sheep-run, but how does Pat Searle fit in there?" Matt asked.

"Pat was already working on the same property in New South Wales, when I got the job there. When I left to come here and landed the job I have now; I asked Pat to come too as they needed more men at the time. So, he came. He knows his job and he is conscientious!"

"Yes, I know, he has proved that. Thank you Herman, I shall never forget your kindness!"

"Any other queries?" Herman asked.

"Just one, young Jeremy wishes to know if his little pal Gerard has also been invited on this picnic. I told him I would ask!" Herman laughed.

"Didn't really give it a thought but that is a good idea – they do seem inseparable – I shall ring his folks and arrange it. Do you think they will let him come along?"

"Leave it to me Herman. I will organize it and have the young chap waiting here at the farm; and thanks once again!"

Jeremy was struggling to lift a bucket of pig-swill into the trough. It was usually the household left-overs, other than meat which was fed to the dogs, and it fell to Jeremy to add some bran and make a swishy swill with plenty of water. Jeremy feared that he had been too liberal with the water and consequently, the bucket was too heavy for the small muscles. Pat Searle approached.

"Hold on there young Jeremy!" He called. "Let me give you a hand before you strain yourself." He did so, the adult muscles making light work of the load.

Pat watched as the son of the house spread the sloppy mash along the length of the trough.

"We have hardly said hello to each other young man, have we?"

"No Sir, Mister Searle – I – I have been busy." Pat nodded as he acknowledged.

"My word yes, you are a very good worker and I have noticed you try and do everything properly. I think that is why Mister Gordon has taken to you; he likes good honest workers."

Jeremy cast a quick look at the hired hand, then looked down, a little embarrassed as he asked.

"Do you really think he likes me?"

"My word he takes you fishing sometimes, he would not do that if he did not like you!"

Jeremy shyly looked up at Pat Searle, and then whispered.

"I like Mister Gordon, and Missus Gordon too, they are real nice to me and Gerard!"

"Well now young Jeremy, I must get back to work. I hope we see a little more of each other; 'bye, have a good day!" Pat sauntered off towards the dairy sheds.

Jeremy ran after him with the empty bucket.

"Mister Searle, excuse me, Mister Searle!"

Pat stopped and waited as the boy came up to him.

"Yes Jeremy?"

"I was just wondering, seeing that Dad is hurt; would you - er – um, do you think you could – er?" The boy bogged down for words.

Pat held out a hand for the bucket. Jeremy passed it to the hired hand and Pat upturned the bucket and sat on it. He beckoned the boy closer; Jeremy came. Pat asked.

"Do you know why your father hired me?"

Jeremy nodded.

"Yes Mister Searle. It was because he is unable to do things and needed help!"

"Exactly! So whatever it is you want, just think of me as your father and I will do those things for him, and for you. Nothing is too much trouble; what is it you want, Jeremy?"

Pat smiled kindly at the embarrassed boy.

"We-ell, Mister Gordon is going to take Gerard and me on a picnic and there may be fishing. It takes a long time to catch yabbies with a string and the little nets we have. I was wondering if you could help me make a big net so it won't be so long getting bait. I wanted to ask my dad but was frightened it might hurt his leg – could you help me please?"

Pat squeezed the boy by his shoulders.

"Ha, is that such a big problem? Come lad, I think if you assist me, we should have a wonderful net in about ten minutes. Come to the storage shed young fellow and we will make it right now!"

Pat had Jeremy find an old chaff bag and undo the seams, while he took a length of fencing wire and fashioned it into a crude circle about one metre in diameter. The opened chaff bag was threaded by the wire, leaving a sagging circular tray. Four potato sack ties were quartered from the wire ring and knotted together by the loose ends. Another piece of cord was tied to the knot.

"There young Jeremy, you just tie some meat scraps in the middle of that and cast it into the dam. After fifteen minutes, just pull the net ashore by the cord and you may pick out the bait-sized yabbies and toss the rest back into the water! How does that suit you?"

Jeremy shook Pat Searle by the hand.

"My word yes, Mister Searle – that is a ripper – thank you!"

He happily raced inside the house with it to show his parents. Pat grinned contentedly to himself.

CHAPTER NINETEEN

The Family Day Picnic

The boys were disappointed when the Gordon's arrived to take them out for the work-related picnic day. Herman asked them to leave their fishing tackle and the live bait at home, as there would be no time for fishing. However, he promised that very soon he would make a special day, just for fishing. He and Moira explained to the children where they were going, and why. Karen, upon hearing about the mother and daughter cooking competition, wanted to know why her mother was not coming along. Moira explained that she was just going to pretend to be her mother, so that Karen could come along to the picnic. That satisfied the seven-year-old. Karen happily went along. The Fisheries and Wildlife Department Picnic Day, was held at a large Nature Reserve on the lower slopes of the ranges, just beyond the headquarters of the department. There were what seemed like hundreds of families attending and the bunting, balloons and side-shows; had the visiting children spellbound.

"Golly! It is almost like the fairgrounds you took us to, Missus Gordon!"

Gerard stated, his blue eyes bright and twinkling; a match for the fairy lights festooning the temporary stalls.

"Will they have fairy floss? I like fairy floss!" Karen asked in awe.

"Yes Dear, I am sure they will." Moira encouraged, contentedly.

Herman drove in to what may be loosely termed as a car park. In reality the area was set aside for the vehicular traffic but being so large and grassy, there was room enough for all patrons to erect their picnic tables beside the cars and set up barbeques. Herman chose a spot beside the rope divider which had pennants dangling, to stop motorists driving through on to the pedestrian area. It gave easy access to that area without risk of the youngsters falling foul of moving vehicles. Also, they could play safely close at hand whilst lunch was being prepared.

"Can we go to the play castle, please?" Jeremy asked of Herman.

"Yes, but wait just a little bit until I get the barbeque set up. I cannot have you three running in all directions – we may never find you again!"

"Yes boys, Moira agreed, we must keep together, and Karen, you stay near me so that you do not get lost in the crowd."

"Oh. I won't get lost. I am seven you know!"

Karen stood akimbo, a severe frown making the adults hide a smile.

"All right, we are all set up; let us look at the displays." Herman announced.

The boys ran ahead, Karen trailing. The Gordon's walked quickly, keeping their enthusiastic charges in sight. The three country minors kicked off their shoes and tumbled into the bouncy, air-filled play castle. Moira and Herman found a niche amongst the many couples watching their off-spring from outside the entrance pylons of the play castle. Over twenty youngsters frolicked and bounced within the high rubber walls, many becoming over-excited, with their parents urgently trying to extract them from the maze of arms and legs. The Gordon's kept a very watchful eye upon the three with whom they were entrusted.

After ten minutes, Herman's stentorian voice boomed over the noisy melee and three very obedient children immediately responded.

"Well done children, was that fun?" He asked as they came bubbling over to their guardians.

"Yes!" The three chorused together.

"I want to have more!" Karen said, her brown eyes the mirror of her brother's, glistened brightly.

"Perhaps after lunch Dear!" Moira suggested. "We will have a quick walk about to see what attractions are here, and then you and I have to make some cakes, while the boys and the fathers have races. The races are at eleven o'clock, so we do not have much time!"

"Oh, goody!"

Herman allowed each of the children to sample one or two side-show attractions. Gerard managed to win a plastic dinosaur on his third throw at the fluffy doll shy, and Jeremy, not to be left out, won a little koopie-doll at the cocoa-nut shy. He immediately gave it to his little sister. Then Karen out-did the boys by looping a plastic quoit over an array of bottles; she won a lovely cuddly stuffed puppy dog.

"Oh! You are so clever dear!"

Moira exclaimed and gave the little girl a kiss upon the forehead. All had a small cup of fruit drink, then the boys and Herman went off to enter the father and son races. Moira and Karen settled down by the camp cooker to prepare some cakes for the cake contest. A deep pot was used as an oven on a very low gas fire. Moira made sweet dampers with a dusting of castor sugar. While that lot were cooking, she had Karen assist in making chocolate crackles. The happy little girl enjoyed mixing the cocoa and sugar with the copra, then spooning the rice bubbles mix into the cake patties. Moira's make-shift apron consisting of a spare tea-towel, showed the enthusiasm of Karen's efforts.

There were many heats of the fifty metres father and son race. Herman ran two heats, with Gerard first and then Jeremy. The third heat, in which Herman had to compete, was Gerard's turn and the two tripped and fell. Herman picked up the youngster and carried him the last twenty metres. They came third and the judge thought about disqualifying the pair but when Herman complained that he ran with a bigger handicap than the other fathers; they were granted the placing. The final was to be Jeremy's turn and he took his place beside his mentor. When the starter's gun was fired, Herman took off with such speed that his little colleague was hard-put to find his footing. Twice Herman bodily lifted the youngster by the scruff of the neck to stop him falling. Jeremy virtually flew over the grass with feet barely touching, because of the powerful man beside him. Both were surprised to find that they were the winners. As the cup with a golden father and son atop of it was awarded to them, Herman let Jeremy hold it as he spoke to the judges. Jeremy wondered what was happening when Herman asked for the cup and tried to hand it back. There was much discussion, with the judges shaking their heads whilst displaying huge smiles upon their faces. The cup was pushed back to Herman and he begrudgingly accepted it, and then let his two wards carry the prize triumphantly back, to show it off to Moira and Karen.

"Dear me boys, I am so proud of you, you must be very fast runners!" Moira encouraged as Karen fingered the figures upon the cup.

"We tried to give it back, as I explained that the two boys were not my sons, but the judges were of the opinion that we won it fairly and squarely and that there were no specific rulings regarding proxy sons. It was all just for fun and enjoyment." Herman told his excited wife.

"Never mind dear, it will not be long before you are a real father!" Moira kissed him.

"Truly?" Jeremy asked, as he overheard.

"So my wife tells me, Jeremy."

"Wow! Won't mum be happy when she hears about this?"

"Settle down young man. Your parents already know, we told them the last time you stayed with us!"

"Oh!"

The boy sounded disappointed that he was unable to be the first to tell his parents the news.

After the picnic barbeque was enjoyed and some of the chocolate crackles were sampled, the children were encouraged to have a half-hour nap. Moira explained that lunch had to be settled first, before they would be allowed to run riot at the fun tents.

Also, the egg and spoon race for children only, was yet to be run. When they woke up, then the fairy-floss could be enjoyed. Karen immediately lay on the blanket provided and the boys followed suit. Moira covered the three with another blanket. The adults then sat on a rug, sipping tea and quietly conversing. A lovely hour of walking the stalls, stopping here and there to watch the activities, sometimes just to fill in time while Moira and Herman chatted with friends and associates; seemed to just fly by. A loud-speaker announced that the time had arrived for the egg and spoon race for children. The under-fours began the contest and the twenty metre run was hilarious for the onlookers. Youngsters not knowing which way to run, even though pointed in the right direction, had their parents give calls of encouragement. One youngster just sat upon the ground with the hard-boiled egg, attempting to crack the egg open with the spoon. When the time came for the seven-year-olds to compete, Karen eagerly jumped about on the starting line, egg in one hand and spoon in the other. Jeremy urged his sister to balance the egg upon the spoon; this she did just as the starter's pistol fired. Gerard yelled.

"Go Karen, go!"

Both boys cheered the little girl on, but alas, the egg bounced out of the spoon and by the time Karen had retrieved the wayward egg; the race was over and won. Disappointed, Karen shuffled back to her group.

"Not to worry Karen, lots of the girls dropped their eggs; anyway, you did win that lovely little puppy-dog!" Moira gave the child a friendly squeeze.

The ten-year-old boys' race with the egg and spoon had the two little cobbers racing against each other. Gerard took off with a huge spurt, only to trip, dislodging his egg. He grabbed the egg mid-air and held it on to the spoon to continue with the race. The stumble was enough for Jeremy to pass him, however the dark curly-haired lad was lucky to scramble past the line in third place. The green ribbon he won had him proudly display the trophy together with the can of drink; which all place-getters received. He shared it with his sister and Gerard.

The announcement for the mother and daughter cooking contest had almost the entire assembly gather about the tables upon which the competing cakes were displayed. As the judges deliberated, there was a general hum of expectation from the eager crowd. Moira's sweet dampers won second prize in the scone-making section. She was over-joyed, as she knew that the competition in that section was fierce. However the surprise for Karen was the 'Honourable Mention' ribbon awarded to her for the chocolate crackles. The little girl's happy face mirrored the pleasure she got from winning her very own ribbon. Moira gave the youngster a congratulatory kiss upon the forehead again.

"Mummy will be so proud of me!" Karen enthused.

Gerard stood with a solemn expression upon his face.

"What is the matter Pal?" Herman asked.

"Aw gee! I am the only one who did not win a soft drink or a ribbon!" The boy sulked.

"Yes, but you did help to win the father and son cup!" Jeremy tried to cheer up his pal.

"But you and Karen got a ribbon and a can of orange drink – I didn't!"

"I shared a can with you." Jeremy said.

"I know. But I don't have a ribbon!" Gerard moped.

"Maybe next time Gerard. Come along Pal, it is not the end of the world."

Herman put a friendly arm about the lad's shoulders.

When the final athletic activities were over, and the Master of Ceremonies had announced a successful day, then thanked all for participating; most families began to pack up and leave.

"I did not get some fairy-floss!" Karen said, with a very downcast face.

"Oh Dear me no!" Moira sympathised. "Let us pack up quickly and have a final look about. I feel sure there will be a vendor still selling fairy-floss!"

With the children keenly helping, the packing up was soon done. The five set forth for a last look at the waning festivities. As the Play Castle was still operating, the three were allowed another five minutes of hilarity; then Herman called his charges off. A fairy-floss vendor was selling his wares to the home-goers, so Herman asked Moira to take the three children there for the promised treat, while he chatted with one of the committee members, who organized the day. When the three youngsters came back to him with Moira, Herman called Gerard aside.

"See that man there?" He asked the boy as he pointed to the man in question.

"Yes Mister Gordon."

"Well, he told me he saw you trip in the heat of the egg and spoon race, but he does not think you deserved a ribbon anyway. I told him that you were a really fast runner and that you should be given another chance!"

Gerard looked back at the man with interest. Herman continued.

"His name is Mullard and he said that if you can run fifty metres in twenty-five seconds, that will prove you are a very good runner and deserve a ribbon. Mister Mullard says it is a waste of time, but if you can run from here to that post; he will award you a ribbon for placing. Do you think you are good enough?"

"My word, of course I can!" Gerard frowned at the man dubiously.

Herman took the boy's fairy-floss and held it for him as Mister Mullard got young Gerard set.

"Go!" He called.

Gerard fairly flew over the fifty metres course. Mister Mullard looked at his stopwatch, a surprised look upon his face as the boy passed the post.

"Crikey!" He breathed. "That is fast for such a little man!"

Mister Mullard had a very serious face as Gerard returned puffing hard. The boy waited, a worried and expectant look bored into the committee man's eyes. Mister Mullard suddenly smiled and extracted a roll of ribbons from the bag he was carrying.

"A really top run, I reckon you would have won the trophy with a run like that – here you are boy – take the ribbon; you truly earned it!"

Gerard's eyes lit up, beacons beaming from the reddened face haloed by his shock of blonde hair.

"Gee thank you Mister Mullard, what about the can of orange juice?"

"Oh dear! Sorry son, we are all out of drinks." He smiled sadly at the boy.

"Not to worry Jack!" Herman grinned. "I shall get one from the freezer for the lad – thanks Jack – see you at the office."

All joined the merry but tired throng as they made their way homewards.

The return journey for the chattering children was a happy one. Each youngster had some memento of their fun-filled day. Moira began humming happily to the sound of the young people in the back seat. Herman joined in and before long, both were singing quietly. Herman, for all of his deep booming voice, sang nicely. The children stopped talking among themselves to listen. Eventually Moira sensed that they were doing so, and began to sing popular songs which she fancied the children would know. The three began to sing with them. One by one,

the tired young people dropped off to sleep. Before they knew it, the children's fun picnic day was over and they had arrived home, to eagerly awaiting parents.

CHAPTER TWENTY

A Woolly Problem

Once again the children settled in to mundane weeks of schooling. Matt was now up and about in earnest, having cast aside one of his crutches to free one hand. Mostly he hopped about everywhere. He felt really good being able to take over the reins of authority with his pickers. Not that there were many left as the apple harvest was all but culminated. One or two of the regular pickers were always retained for an extra few months for pruning, cultivating and the annual servicing of the orchard; which was necessary for the following year's harvest.

Pat Searle was due to leave in two days to begin his regular rounds with the Fisheries and Game Department. He was looking forwards to 'the rest', as he termed it. While he still had the services of Pat, Matt utilised the man in driving him all over the farm. Matt needed to inspect his holdings just to assure himself that nothing heavy had to be attended; while he still had an able-bodied man in tow. Just a few odd things such as a fallen limb on a fence, and a hole where a wombat had dug under a strainer post, needed to be addressed. It was as well Matt made the decision to use Pat, as he would never have been able to remove the branch alone. Matt had one final duty for Pat before he left, and that was to assist with the drenching of the sheep. While Pat held each sheep so that Matt could apply the dose, Matt whistled his dogs to hold the sheep in close. They were already in the home holding pen but needed to be kept bunched up for easy selection. As each animal was drenched, Pat scrambled it through the race to freedom in the home paddock. When all were done, Pat opened the home paddock gate, then Matt had Sam and Bluey muster the noisy herd out into the open pastures. It was a thankful couple of owners who settled their account with Pat Searle and wished him well on his return to the normal occupations of his working life. Pat asked his temporary employers if they would pass on to their children, a couple of gifts that he had fashioned for them. This Matt and Yvonne promised that they would do – with thanks! Karen was over-joyed to receive a cuddly little doll that Pat had fashioned for her, after it had been cleaned and dyed, from the tailings of their own sheep. Jeremy gazed in awe at the workmanship of a dainty riding-crop that Pat had plaited himself.

"It is only for show, Dad!" The serious brown-eyed lad explained. "I would never use it to whip Bessie; she is too well-behaved and obedient. Isn't it a beauty though?"

Herman and his men were back on the job. He had paired up with the other man doing the rounds of his protectorate, leaving Pat the responsibility of travelling to headquarters to pick up stores and equipment, needed to maintain the services they were paid to provide. Pat was on the return journey with the council van loaded to over-flowing. It was sagging well down on its ample springs. Pat stopped to check that his load had not shifted; with the back door raised as he leaned in to the body of the vehicle. An approaching one-tonne cattle truck came to a noisy stop on the road opposite him. The driver, a balding scraggly-haired man of some thirty years, who was wearing ill-fitting spectacles which threatened to fall off his nose; called out to the man whom he could scarcely see amongst the load in his van.

"Oy! Which road do I take to Berrilla?"

Pat left what he was doing and crossed the road to save shouting. He stood by the driving-side door of the cattle-truck, which had a load of lambs aboard.

"Keep going about two kilometres then turn left at the bitumen road. It is only one kilometre from there to the junction. Berrilla is twenty kilometres to the right on the second turn-off!"

"Thanks mate!" The driver called as he drove away.

Pat idly looked at the tagged sheep as the truck moved away. He recognised the tags and fancied he saw the name 'Purcell', stamped upon one of them. 'Must have picked up a load off Matt'! He mused. His trained eye caught the vehicle number plate. Pat wrote the number down on a pad he took from his shirt pocket. A telephone call from his mobile 'phone to his temporary employer, confirmed that Matt had not sold any of his stock since Pat had worked for him. Immediately the authorities were contacted and the details wired off to them of the truck, the man driving it and the tags the stolen sheep would be wearing. Pat about turned his vehicle and attempted to catch up with the suspect truck and driver. Alas, his over-laden van was no match for the truck and it was too far away by the time Pat arrived at the junction. He decided to leave the chase to the proper authorities. Matt had Yvonne drive him to Berrilla, the asked for destination of the cattle-truck, in which Matt's lambs were reportedly seen. The possibility of course, was that Berrilla was not the true destination of the stolen stock! Perhaps that township was only a guide for the driver to get onto the right highway. Matt asked his wife to hasten a little more.

"The speeding fine may cost more than the sheep are worth, Dear; let us be careful!"

"Yes. You are right. Dash the rotters anyway; I wonder why they picked our farm?"

Yvonne had what she thought was the answer.

"I think it was that sale of lambs we just sent in; they did bring a very good price!"

"Yes. I dare say someone who checked the buyers slip would have access to that knowledge, I have got really good quality lambs this year." Matt agreed.

"This is Berrilla coming up now dear, which way do I drive?" Yvonne asked.

143

"Straight through, there should be a Service Station just out of town. If the cattle truck has gone through, someone at the Service Station may have noticed it. It will be best to ask there!"

Yvonne stopped her sedan at the Service Station office. Matt entered and conversed with the attendant.

"No! He says that if a cattle truck went through in the last hour, he would have noticed it. None have gone through!"

"Perhaps they turned off somewhere!" Yvonne suggested.

Matt and Yvonne drove around the local streets. They toured the back streets of the small hamlet for a good half hour. It was pure luck that Yvonne saw truck tyre marks at the intersection of a small cross-road. A truck had hit a pot-hole as the truck turned the corner, leaving quite distinct wheel marks. The damning evidence that it may have been the truck they were seeking was the sprinkling of sheep-droppings strewn along the tyre marks. The Purcell's hurriedly drove in pursuit. Two kilometres along this back road, the two sleuths found a cattle truck unloading at the rear of a property. Matt had Yvonne stop the sedan and they watched. Matt rang his local Police Station asking for the assistance of the local constabulary at Berrilla – there was none! A couple of detectives would come from Matt's home town. As they would take up to a half hour to get there, it was suggested that Matt stay put, observing, in the event that the cattle truck was just delivering and may take off; then Matt could follow at a distance. The cattle truck stayed where it was for nearly a half hour, presumably so that payment could be finalised and possibly the driver may have been invited to stay for a few drinks. The driver quit the house and started his cattle truck. As the engine roared into life, Matt had Yvonne drive the sedan across the gate way to block the truck from leaving. The driver of the cattle truck sounded his horn for the sedan to move. Matt alighted from the car and hopped over to speak to the driver.

"Yeah! What's the idea?" The man demanded.

Matt saw that the man fitted the description of the driver whom Pat spoke to and the number-plate tallied, so he stalled for time; hoping that the police would arrive sooner rather than later.

"Just wondering what you would charge to take twenty-five lambs from the saleyards to my property?" Matt queried.

"Eh?" The driver was startled, no doubt as that was the exact amount of sheep he had just delivered.

"It would be about twenty kilometres each way." Matt pushed.

"I have just finished for the day – get out of the way!" The man ordered.

"Surely you can let me know what it will cost. I see you just unloaded around that amount, you must have a good idea about the cost!" Matt kept pressing.

"Sixty five bucks, now move your car, I have to get back!"

Matt turned and hopped back to the sedan then appeared to recall something and again hopped over to the truck driver.

"Oh! One last thing - !!"

The driver revved his engine and moved forwards as if to ram the sedan; Yvonne shrieked. Matt brandished his crutch ready to smash the truck windscreen and the angry driver stopped, centimetres from the sedan.

"Move your rotten car or I'll ram you!" He shouted.

The melee caused the occupants of the house to approach. There were three surly types with a scruffy looking woman trailing them.

"What's going on?"

The largest of the men called. He was a huge man who wore only decrepit jeans and a streaky singlet. His stomach threatened to break through, no doubt encouraged by the beer he seemed to have a liking for, as one hand held a beer can. The men surrounded Matt and Yvonne, who was still sitting in the sedan.

"What do you want?" The big man asked, belligerently.

"He asked me what it costs to take twenty-five sheep from the saleyards to his property and he won't move his damned car!" The driver of the truck informed.

"Twenty-five huh?" The big man looked threateningly at the intruders. "Why for twenty-five?" He asked.

"The truck seemed capable of taking that amount and that is all I wish to move!" Matt said, in as casual a manner as he could.

"Something fishy here!" The big man threatened as he closed in on Matt.

A siren sounded and all realized that a police car had sneaked up on them unnoticed. Matt breathed a sigh of relief as things were beginning to get sticky. All awaited the arrival of a detective and a uniformed policeman.

"Hello Matt!" The detective greeted. "Got your facts straight?"

"Yes Clive. The description and number plate tally. I have not seen the sheep or the tags yet though. Those may be the ones in the holding pen there, they have just been unloaded!"

The detective identified himself and the uniformed officer, and then demanded of the driver and the other man.

"Names please!"

They were told of the suspicions, and after confirmation that the sheep were indeed 'duffed' from the Purcell property; all were read their rights and charged. The men were ordered to re-load the stock back into the cattle truck and the truck was then taken into custody as police evidence. The uniformed officer drove the stolen stock back to the Purcell farm.

That evening at home, Matt and Yvonne relived the day's happenings as they informed Jeremy and Karen of the duffing.

"Wow!" Jeremy breathed in awe. "Wish I didn't have to be at school that would have been great fun chasing sheep duffers!"

"Did the men hurt our sheep Daddy?" Karen asked.

"No Karen, not at all they just took them for a ride." Her father quelled her fears.

"The reason that we told you about the men stealing our sheep is so that you understand that the bad people always get caught. You must never take things that do not belong to you. If these bad men do not go to jail, then they will have to pay a very big fine!" Yvonne stressed.

"We do not take things Mummy, we are not thieves!" Karen spoke out peremptorily.

"Yes Dear, I know. That is one reason why mummy and daddy love you both so much."

"Dad!"

"Yes Son?"

"How did you know where to find the men who stole our sheep?" Jeremy sat wide eyed. His interest in the matter of great moment to him, for the episode would be a great subject for conversation at school.

"It was Mister Searle, Jeremy. Had we not employed him, then he may not have recognised our tags on the lambs. We have to thank him for being so observant. He took the truck number and wrote it down, and then he rang me to find out if I had sold any sheep lately."

"But you did Dad. Mister Searle helped you to market!" Jeremy exclaimed.

"Yes, that is true, but that was almost two weeks ago. Those lambs would be well and truly out of the district by now, so if lambs are about with my tags on them, there is a good chance that they were stolen!"

Jeremy considered this little gem of information, and then deliberated.

"I like Mister Searle. He helped me make that beaut yabby net and he made a terrific riding crop for me!" As Matt nodded, his son continued.

"Mister Searle has to be a nice man because Mister Gordon would not work with him otherwise!"

"You really like Mister Gordon, don't you Jeremy?" Yvonne smiled.

"Gosh! I'll say Mum. He takes me to his best fishing spots and he teaches me lots of things. And Gerard and me have been on picnics and we stayed at his sister's place and all!" Jeremy enthused.

"Yes Dear." Yvonne agreed. "He has been very good to all of us!"

"Yeah! And he saved my life when I fell down into the pit up on the ranges – he is my very best friend – after Gerard!"

Matt had been thinking as his wife and son were reminiscing.

"Do you know what I think?" Both Jeremy and his mother turned to the head of the house.

"No Dear, what do you think?" Yvonne asked.

"I really think we should do something very nice for Mister Gordon. He has been good to us and for us!"

"Yes Dad. I would love to do something nice for Mister Gordon! What can we do that is nice?" Jeremy keenly listened for his father's suggestion.

"They will be parents themselves soon!" Yvonne reminded.

"Yes Dear, I had that in mind." Matt nodded as he thought aloud. "Everyone, family, friends, neighbours – all will be giving baby clothes – bassinets, prams, pushers, nappies etcetera. I think we should try to find something different; something to remember us by that will last!"

"Hey Daddy I know!" Jeremy jumped up and ran to his room. Matt looked quizzically at Yvonne. Her blank look and shrugged shoulders, matched his own ignorance of the boy's act. Jeremy returned triumphantly, waving some photographs.

"There Daddy – see?" His parents looked.

"Your baby photographs and a couple from your holiday at Aunt Jane's, do you think we should send them photographs, Son?" Yvonne asked sceptically.

"No! But we should get them a nice camera to take pictures of the baby and maybe a really nice Photo Album!" Jeremy beamed at his parents; they exchanged glances.

"What a grand idea Son!" His father applauded.

CHAPTER TWENTY ONE

The Rescuers

It was on the Saturday morning, three weeks after the three children had been on the family day picnic with Herman and Moira Gordon, that Jeremy and Gerard set forth on one of the usual fishing trips to their peninsular. The Gordon's had not been heard from and Matt was due to have his plastered ankle freed, in fact he was actually walking unaided having discarded the crutches. Yvonne made sure that her son packed the cellular telephone before setting off for the day. A cut lunch and drinks safely tucked into his creel with the telephone, had Jeremy feel ready for any adventure which may happen along. Gerard too, was similarly equipped, although he did not have the luxury of a personal telephone. His parents deeming that one between the two boys to be ample safeguard. It was as well the boys did have recourse to this handy life-saving device. Having had very good fishing with Herman Gordon, the peninsular was beginning to feel 'old hat' to both boys.

"Why don't we try some new place for fishing?" Jeremy asked.

"S'pose we could!" Gerard agreed. "I am getting a bit sick of the peninsular and anyway, the spots there are getting to be fished out. Where else can we go?"

Jeremy considered the options.

"We have not been to the falls since the day Dad took us last year."

"Crikey! You know that is five kilometres away and we have already ridden six, well I have, from my place to yours and then to here; we may get home late and cop a punishment!" Gerard warned.

"If you are not too tired, we can do it." Jeremy urged.

"Don't know if we are supposed to go that far. My dad thinks I am just at the river and that's all!" Gerard worried.

"Where else is there that is different? We have been to all the spots upstream and Mister Gordon does not want us in his very special peninsular alone. Another thing, downstream is scrubby and the river goes ever away from the road. The next best place downstream is only the falls; there is nowhere else – let's do it!"

"All right I s'pose!" Gerard reluctantly agreed.

The two boys cycled along the road to Fletcher's Falls.

Although the area was very much virgin bushland, there were many open glades and good grassy banked spots along the edge for fishing. The falls itself was only a ten metres drop but because of the rocky terrain, the noise was a constant roar. One had to almost shout to be heard. The boys settled down to their fishing, some two hundred metres from the cascade, where the frothy water began to subside somewhat; at a shallow sandy inlet. Each lad took up a position at either side of the inlet, just where the water was darker and a little deeper. Sitting under trees and behind scrub-grasses, hidden from the sight of any cruising fish which may be lurking about, the boys patiently awaited the first bite. The calm and serenity of this idyllic setting lulled the youngsters into a dreamy state, which a nibble to their lines would have immediately dispersed. There were no preliminary bites. Above the constant roar of the waterfall, a dull thud was heard.

"What was that?" Gerard asked.

"Yes. I thought I heard something. It sounded like it came from near the falls!" Jeremy confirmed.

"Think we should go and have a look?" Gerard queried.

"It was probably just a tree going over the top." Jeremy sounded uninterested.

"I'd like to go and see, anyway. Come on!" Gerard began to reel in his line.

"Oh all right!" Jeremy followed suit. The boys rode back to the cascade.

"Wow! Someone has crashed into the water!"

Gerard yelled, as the pair came within sight of the basin below the falls. A half-cabin truck was nose down in the water with the rear wheels just holding on the bank.

"If there is anyone in it, they must be drowned. Look, the water is in the cabin. Let's hurry!" Jeremy gasped as he left his bicycle and gear near the mishap.

"It is a council truck. It is not Mister Gordon's though!" Gerard cried dramatically.

"We had better look in the cabin in case someone is still in it!" Jeremy advised, then, tentatively. "You stay there, I will have a look!"

The boy scrambled into the water up to his neck. He could barely see inside the cabin as he swam to the stricken vehicle. When he grabbed hold of the door catch, the vehicle groaned and subsided slightly. Jeremy gave a startled shriek.

"Get away, it will sink and drag you down with it!" Gerard urgently called from the bank.

"I can't, there is someone still in it, and I can see him. I think he's dead!" Jeremy screamed.

"Come and help, we have to get him out!"

The boy strained to open the door. It was stuck but opened to the frantic efforts of the determined lad. He reached into the vehicle and unbuckled the safety harness, then pulled the body towards himself, downstream. Gerard suddenly splashed in beside him and together they tugged the body out of the truck.

"Aw, Crikey!" Jeremy began sobbing. "It is Mister Searle – quick, pull hard – he might not be dead. Come on Gerard, try harder!"

Blood was trickling from a gash on the man's right forehead, no doubt where his head came into violent contact with the metal upright of the door-jamb.

"We will never be able to lift him out of the water, he is too heavy!" Gerard grizzled. "What should we do?"

"I will ring for help. Can you hold him if I get out?" Jeremy asked.

"Yeah! I think so. Who will you ring? My dad went to the market and your dad still has a crook leg?"

"Mister Gordon. He can save Mister Searle and he has a winch to rescue the truck!" The youngster quickly found his telephone, and reading the number on his creel, rang his hero, Herman Gordon. Herman's deep voice cheerily asked.

"Who is it?"

"It is Jeremy Mister Gordon. Mister Searle is dead, he has drowned!" He burst out crying.

"What? Jeremy, don't go making bad jokes boy!"

"I am not! His truck is crashed into the pool at Fletcher's Falls and we can't get him out of the water; he is too heavy!" The sobbing poured forth.

"All right Son, just calm down or we can't be any help. Is there any blood, is he breathing?"

"His head is cut and bleeding but Mister Searle is in the water, Gerard is holding him so he won't float away but we can't get him up on the bank!"

"All right Jeremy, now listen to me – are you listening?"

"Yes!"

"Can you put your face by his mouth and feel if he is breathing? If he is, wash his face with water, he may wake up. Do you understand boy?"

"Yes Mister Gordon."

"Oh, and Jeremy!"

"Yes?"

"Put your hand on his heart, you may feel it beating."

"Yes Mister Gordon."

"Do not switch the 'phone off, I am on my way. I am just at the shack – keep calm son!" Jeremy did as he was bid.

"What is happening, was Mister Gordon home, is he coming?" Gerard asked, frightened that he may be holding a dead body.

"He is coming but we have to wash Mister Searle's face and feel his heart!" Jeremy obeyed the instructions he was given. "I can't feel any breathing and I don't know if I have my hand where his heart is – I will wash his face!"

Jeremy splashed and patted water on the face of the man they were supporting. There was no response.

"He sure must be dead!" Jeremy sobbed. Gerard too, began to sniffle.

"I liked Mister Searle; he gave me a nice riding crop that he made!" Jeremy cried.

Herman Gordon drove his four wheel drive to a sliding stop and raced over to the dramatic scene.

"Right boys; push him over so that I can grab him!"

They did so and Herman easily hoisted the limp form up onto the grassy bank and applied resuscitation. There was a heartbeat but it was very faint and breathing commenced. Pat Searle remained unconscious. A siren could be heard rapidly approaching and very soon an ambulance stopped near Herman's vehicle. The medical staff immediately and very efficiently, moved into action and within minutes, Pat Searle was whisked away to intensive care. Herman consoled the two sobbing children.

"Mister Searle is being properly looked after boys. He is alive and I think he will be all right. You did well to save him and I think you are both very brave boys, you may very well be the ones who have saved his life."

"He is not dead then?" Gerard asked, tearfully.

"No, but he is a very ill man!"

"Will he die but?" Jeremy tugged at Herman's sleeve to gain attention.

"The ambulance medico's say he has a very good chance of surviving, it just depends upon how much water he may have swallowed.

"Can we go to the hospital and visit him? I don't want Mister Searle to die!" Jeremy hung his head, crestfallen.

"Not until he is getting better. Come lads, we will put you in my car and I will take you home."

A police car pulled alongside just as Herman was about to drive on to the gravel road.

"Hello Herman, couldn't wait, huh?" The driver called.

"Take your photo's and measurements Ken, I will catch up with you later at the Police Station – have to get the boys home – they are sopping wet. I will have their parents come in with them for statements, okay?"

The police officer nodded, then drove down to the stricken vehicle. Herman drove the two sad boys' home. Percy and Grace Lonard hurried over to the Purcell's farm, when Matt rang to explain the circumstances which led to Gerard being showered and then outfitted in some of Jeremy's clothing.

"We thought it best to get the boys out of their saturated clothing as soon as possible!"

"But of course. Oh Yvonne, thank you so much. The poor, brave little dears; what a fright they must have had!"

Percy turned to Herman who had just placed the telephone receiver upon its cradle.

"What is the condition of Mister Searle; will he survive?"

Herman had a whimsical smile on his face as he answered.

"That was the hospital I just contacted!"

He actually beamed all around at the gathering in the Purcell kitchen, as he made the announcement.

"Pat is doing very well. It seems that he hardly swallowed any water – thanks to the quick actions of your boys – and his only injury is the crack on the head he received, when the truck bounced off the tree which sent him into the river. He is heavily concussed but has regained consciousness. Pat will be all right!"

"Thank goodness for that!" Yvonne sighed for all.

Gerard and Jeremy came into the kitchen, faces still glum.

"Thank goodness for what, Mum?" Jeremy asked.

"Oh Jeremy! Come give mum a cuddle, we have some good news for you both. Mister Searle is getting better and has woken up. He will be fine, thanks to you two boys. You probably saved his life when you stopped him from drowning. I am so proud of you my Son!"

"Well done boys!" Matt reached out and warmly shook both boys by the hand.

"Hot chocolate?" Grace offered a steaming cup to Gerard and Jeremy; the glum faces had brightened appreciatively.

"Any idea how Pat came to crash into the tree?" Percy asked of Herman.

"Ken rang his man at the hospital to find out Pat's condition and he mentioned to him that it may be that the brakes failed. There was a long streak of brake fluid leading to the tree. The fluid line seems to have come unstuck or maybe it was torn off by a strong bush. That appears to be the most logical cause at the moment. Ken reported that there was no sign of another vehicle being involved!"

"When can we visit Mister Searle, Mum?" Jeremy asked.

"Let him rest quietly today and tomorrow Dear. I will keep in touch with the hospital and maybe at lunch-time on Monday, we will see if the teacher will let you visit then. It all depends on whether the doctor says you can; Mister Searle may not be able to have visitors too soon. Just be patient Jeremy!"

"I want to go too!" Gerard exclaimed.

"Yes Gerard, you will go too!" Grace assured her son.

Monday morning had nearly passed. Gerard and Jeremy found that they were 'clock watching' during the last lesson before the lunch break. Miss Purdie, their teacher, was summoned to the class room door, by the Principal. He was accompanied by a Senior Police Officer of the district. All conversed in the passageway for a minute or so, then Miss Purdie called Gerard and Jeremy out of the classroom. The boys already knew the Principal, so were introduced to Captain Stuart Longford of the district Police Headquarters.

"So, these are the brave quick-thinkers! How are you boys?"

The two acknowledged the officer's attention and answered.

"Good, thank you."

"I have come to take you to see Mister Searle in Hospital. He has been asking when he can see you. Your parents are already there and Herman Gordon is waiting in my car to come with us. You would like to visit Mister Searle, wouldn't you?"

"Yes please, Captain Longford!" Both boys replied.

"Come along then, I need to ask you just a couple of questions about the accident and Mister Gordon volunteered to act as your witness to my questions, in lieu of your parents. Is that okay?"

"Yes Sir!"

At the hospital the boys were very surprised to see that Pat Searle was sitting up in bed, a bandage encircling his head. The parents of both lads were seated at either side of the bed and besides nurses and a doctor, there was an official dignitary. He was Alderman Mason, the Lord Mayor, wearing his official chain of office. Each boy went to the side of the bed where his parents were sitting with proud expressions upon their faces.

"Hello young Jeremy and Gerard, come let me shake your hands!" Pat welcomed the boys. They came and they shook hands, cameras clicked. Surprised at the gathering, the boys became quiet.

"Shake hands again please – just one more shot!" A photographer pleaded.

Pat gave each boy another handshake, this time pulling the boys close and whispering to them.

"Thank you boys, I am your friend for life!"

Embarrassed, they pulled away to seek comfort from their parents. Captain Longford asked the boys to come forwards to the end of the bed, where Lord Mayor Mason shook the boy's hands and each was awarded a Civic Medal for Bravery, on behalf of the City and its citizens. Then Herman Gordon gave both boys a Fisheries and Gaming lapel badge, for valuable services on behalf of the Fisheries and Gaming Department. The photographers had a field day. After a short speech by the Police Captain, praising the lads for their prompt action and courageous behaviour; most of the dignitaries and the hospital staff departed. Only the boys, their parents, Herman and one nurse, remained. Jeremy and Gerard proudly showing off their awards to their parents were once again called to Pat's bedside; by the happily smiling man.

"I wonder if I too, could see your awards boys." He asked.

The two obliged and after Pat ruffled each boy's hair in turn, he vowed.

"If ever you need a friend, if ever you need someone to just talk to, or if ever you get into trouble; just give me a ring on the telephone. I have asked your parents if it is all right to do so and they have my number. I owe my life to your quick thinking and the fact that you were there just when I needed you the most. I meant what I said before boys. I am your best friend, for life. Thanks boys!"

CHAPTER TWENTY TWO

Jane Returns

The rest of the week was a happy time for the two rescuers. Their close mates revered them and the Head Master officially praised the boys at the following morning's roll-call; in front of all the children attending the school. The boys had their names placed upon a special honour-roll in the corridor, just outside the Head Master's office; including a clipping of the local paper's write-up of the event. The two boys were allowed to visit Pat Searle at the hospital after school each day for the rest of that week. The three became very good friends. Pat was released from the hospital after one week. He returned to light duties at his place of employment. Life for all carried on as normal, and once more the community settled down to the sameness of every day living. Matt was relieved to at last have the plaster cast removed and began to move about the farm and orchard with gusto. The fruit picking had finished and the Purcell's awaited their due cheques with a feeling of well-being for a season's work well done; especially so after the many happenings over the past half year. Matt and Yvonne settled comfortably of an evening with their children asleep and healthy, giving thanks for their satisfying state of affairs; both marital and financially. The Lonard's too, had also been blessed with a successful season with both vineyard and market gardens. Gerard was enjoying life with his best cobber Jeremy, and the boy's associations with Herman Gordon, seemed to have brought out the better qualities of both children. The proud parents blessed their lucky stars for the contented way their lives were progressing. The Lonards' daughter Leanne was their only concern, in that she was approaching fourteen years of age and they dreaded the 'terrible teens' time, now at hand. Leanne was already infatuated by one of her High School friends and although he was, as they saw him, 'a very nice boy', he too was a teenager and as good parents, they worried.

A happy man was Herman Gordon. His Moira was beginning to show the signs of her pregnancy and was glowing in health, both physical and mental. The two were still as love-birds in that they doted upon each other, and the blessed event could not seem to come soon enough. Preliminary tests showed that they may expect twins.

"I wonder if one will have curly black hair and the other one straight blonde." Herman joked.

"Wouldn't that be a treat?"

"I do not like the chances dear!" Moira smiled as she kissed her man. "They may be two girls, you know!" Moira warned.

"So what?" Herman cuddled his wife and patted her pregnancy. "Two little wonders like Karen would be stupendous. In any case, even if they are one of each, they would be ours – our very own – and we will not have the heart-ache of returning them after a day's outing. We can tuck them into their own beds in our comfy little home!" He again kissed Moira. "Did I tell you how beautiful you are and that I love you very much?"

They subsided on the settee, fondly embracing.

Jane de Lune paid a surprise visit to the Purcell home. It was just after the evening meal and dusk was giving way to nightfall, when her sedan came to a stop at the front verandah. With pleasant surprise, Matt invited Jane into the house.

"Why, Jane! How nice of you to call, please sit down and I will make a cuppa!"

Yvonne whisked off to the kitchen, leaving her visitor to talk with Matt. Jeremy could be heard to ask.

"Do we have a visitor, Mum?"

He appeared in the doorway with Karen hurrying after him, both in their night attire.

"Oh! Hello children!" Jane gushed. "My brother told me how brave you were to rescue Mister Searle. Dear me Jeremy, we are all so proud of you!"

"Yes'm – thank you."

Jeremy was showing signs of his actions beginning to become boring conversation. Noticing this, Jane turned her attention to Karen.

"Karen Dear, I have some very nice news for you and your mum!"

"True?"

"Yes Dear – oh – here is your mother now. Yvonne, sorry to blow in on you unannounced, but I was just bursting with my news and as I was so near here, I -!!"

"Stuff and nonsense Jane, you do not need an invite; the door is always open to you. But we are intrigued, what is this good news?"

Jane took a sip from the cup provided, before answering. She grandiosely and carefully extracted a framed certificate from her carry-bag.

"Look there – just read that – I am so thrilled!"

She passed the certificate over for all to read in turn.

'First prize in the Berrilla Art Show?' Yvonne read in wonder. 'Jane de Lune!'" Yvonne exclaimed in awe. "Why Jane, how delightful. Why did you not tell me, I would have attended?"

"Oh dear! I am sorry. I never thought you were that interested but now I wish that I had told you." Jane seemed a little abashed.

"How is that?" Yvonne asked.

"This!" Jane took out a green ribbon from her carry-bag. She handed it to Karen.

"Thank you Aunt Jane. Is it for me?" Karen fondled the ribbon in wonderment.

"Yes Karen, can you read it?"

The little girl stretched the ribbon out upon the floor, and then jumped up, sharply calling.

"Mummy, Mummy, it has my name on it!"

"Really Karen, are you sure?"

Yvonne took the ribbon offered for her inspection and read it aloud. 'Berrilla Art Show, Special Effort Award to Karen Purcell in the Novice Section!' Yvonne turned puzzled eyes to Jane for an explanation.

"I do hope you don't mind Yvonne, but as I had to put three of my Bark Paintings in, I thought I may just as well enter the one Karen gave me; in the junior section. I put it under her name, because after all, it is her work and I thought it had special merit for a seven-year-old. Well, so did the judges and there you have it. I hope I did not take too much liberty!"

"Oh Jane, how sweet of you!" Yvonne rose and kissed the older lady's cheek. "I am so thrilled. Karen, your bark picture won a Special Award. You know the one you gave to Aunt Jane – say 'thank you'!"

With bright eyes and a very big smile, Karen ran to Aunt Jane and gave her a sloppy kiss.

"Thank you for teaching me Aunt Jane, do you want to see my other pictures too?"

"Of course Aunt Jane does dear, she may as well see mine too!"

The three females left the room, leaving Matt and Jeremy alone.

"Golly Son, it looks like we have a budding artist in our midst now. What with all of these awards my family are receiving, I feel like a piece of stonework just lying about!"

Matt reached for his son. The boy wrapped his arms about his father's neck, saying.

"Wish I could give you an award for being the best father in the world. I love you Daddy - so does Karen!"

Matt squeezed the little body to him. A tear threatened to dampen his vision. His throat seemed to lump up.

"Your dad loves you and Karen so much too. Mum and I are very proud of you both! Do you think we should go and see what the ladies are doing?"

Jeremy struggled to sit on his father's knees.

"Nah! I just want to sit here with you, Dad!"

Matt slightly hugged his son to him and kissed the boy's curly hair.

Jane de Lune stayed for two hours. Every time she attempted to leave, either Karen or Yvonne would ask another question relating to the bark picture hobby. It was left to Matt to rescue her by preparing supper; his motivation was that the children were long overdue to be in bed, asleep. Jane insisted on tucking the two in and gave each a light kiss on the forehead. At last the three adults were settled in the kitchen and the topic was still, bark pictures.

"You know what I think?"

Matt said, as he studied a shortbread biscuit he was contemplating, with the intent to eventually devour it.

"No Dear, but I am intrigued!" Yvonne flippantly responded.

"Seeing that you are jealous of our daughter's expertise and her apparently superior artistic talent - !!"

"Now just you be very careful Matt. I am the cook you know!" Yvonne cut her man short. Matt ignored her and continued.

"I think we should invite Jane to stay for a week, just to get you up to Karen's standard!"

"Well! Of all the gall! No – not the invite Jane – that is a splendid idea. Would you consider it? Oh I would love to have you at hand for instruction. My husband does come up with some grand ideas. Please Jane, do come and stay for a week. We have some wonderful trees for the bark we need around here. You saw the pieces Matt and Jeremy got for us the day they pushed a tree on themselves!"

Jane promised to come in one week's time, declaring it to be a God-send and a relief from the sameness of her everyday, sometimes lonely, life. She would enjoy being in the company of the two lively children again, doing that one thing in life that she loved, to relax her boredom; bark picture making!

"It is always nice to find someone else who is a kindred spirit. I shall groom you to win in next year's Art Show at Berrilla!" Jane promised. She drove away in a very happy and fulfilled frame of mind.

Mid-morning on the following day, Yvonne called to her man as he was painting one of the sheds. "Pat Searle is on the 'phone Dear!"

"Coming." He called.

"Just as well he did or I would never have got you away from the painting. There is tea made, so don't be long!"

When Matt sat at the table to partake of the tea and cake prepared for him, he was shaking his head.

"What is it dear, is Pat recovering well?"

"Better than that, Yvonne, he is one hundred percent he tells me but the Fisheries and Game will not take the risk of him working, after the concussion. They have given Pat one month sick leave on full pay, which is inclusive of the week he has already spent in hospital. The department paid all of his medical expenses, as it is covered by insurance and so is the months' rest and recreation. It is called 'recovery period', he was told!"

"I see, so what did he call about? He has already thanked the boys!" Yvonne was sceptical.

"I believe he feels that he needs to give something back to the boys. He has offered his services for light duties for a week – to help Jeremy – he says. He is also going to offer the same to the Lonards!"

"But that is so unnecessary. Jeremy has been over-indulged now. I do not think that will help the boy!" Yvonne worried.

"I have already expressed that and do you know what he answered?"

"No – surprise me!"

"He said it won't do any harm but he needs to do it to help him! Pat feels that he owes his life to the boys and would like to do little things for them, and the best way for him to help the boys, is by helping their parents. He has three idle weeks and his heart is breaking. He has to be busy!"

Pat Searle returned for one week to do light work for one week on half pay. The money, he insisted, was incidental. As he was already on full pay, Pat would have pottered about for no pay at all. That Matt and Yvonne were contributing a little, made for a more comfortable relationship all round. He and Matt managed to get done many menial tasks, which more often than not, were overlooked because of their incidentiality. Uncharacteristically, Jeremy seemed a little shy whenever he and Pat crossed paths. Pat studiously avoided any reference to the mishap at the river, in an attempt to put the youngster at ease. After school on the last day Pat was to work at the farm, Jeremy was most surprised to find Pat with curry-comb in hand and Bessie resplendent with a glossy coat and well-brushed mane and tail.

"Gosh Mister Searle, doesn't Bessie look beautiful? Thanks!"

"I just thought she could do with a brush-up. Would you have time to help me do her shoes?"

"My word I would, shall I get the blacking?" He hurried to do so.

Pat patiently held each of Bessie's hooves aloft for her owner to clean them and apply the shiner. The boy proudly walked Bessie around her yard. Jeremy's beaming face showing his great pleasure as Pat watched and appreciated the boy's happiness.

"I am going to show Bessie off to mum and dad, will you come with me." He asked of Pat. When Pat left the Purcell farm, he headed straight for the home of Percy and Grace Lonard; to do a similar service for them in deference to Gerard's part in his rescue.

Pat's departure signalled the arrival of Jane de Lune, for the promised week's break from her home and the beginning of her tutorial expertise in the area of Bark Picture making. The while that Karen was at school and with Jane assisting with domestic duties, the two ladies found ample time to pursue with gusto, their hobby. After Karen had completed her home-work – which was always despatched immediately the girl returned from school – lessons in bark picture making commenced. Jeremy found time to do many of the smaller tasks which normally fell to his little sister. In this he was heartily praised by both his parents and indeed, by 'Aunt Jane' too! The children were denied the many forays into the scrubland, as the ladies foraged for barks that were suitable to their hobby. School took of the children's time. The house was changing so far as the inner décor was concerned. Every room had one or two of the hobby pictures adorning the walls. There were also a dozen or so of the bark pictures put aside for the next exhibition, to be held at the Art Society. Karen and her mother were agog with excitement and found the time dragging until the next year's showing would eventuate.

"We will just have to hold our own Art Show!" Jane decided.

"Oh what a grand idea!" Yvonne applauded. "Where do you suggest we should do that?"

"What about the local school?" Jane whimsically asked. Yvonne clapped her hands.

"Beautiful, and so opportune too!"

"How so?" Jane was intrigued.

"Parents and Teachers Day! It is to be held at the end of the month – a Monday. As I am on the committee, I shall suggest a mini-exhibition and with a little luck, who knows, we may just sell one or two!"

"Oh gorgeous! Let us amass a few really good quality pictures and before we know it, the whole school may be attracted to the hobby!" Jane enthused.

"What do we call these pictures? I seem to remember them being referred to as 'Bark Paintings'. But they are really pictures, aren't they?" Yvonne asked.

Jane was off-handed with her answer.

"Who knows? To me they are truly 'pictures' but when all of the more strident dark and light barks are used, especially when one has a thick glaze to seal them; I feel they are more like 'paintings'. In any case, they are a wonderful hobby and a delight to look upon!" Yvonne idly confessed.

"I am going to be hard-put to part with any of them."

Jane concurred, and then teased.

"Just wait until you see the money pouring in, then you will quickly change your mind. You know –" Jane confided "- I have gathered quite a large sum from the sale of my pictures. Mainly through the agency of the different Art Shows, then word-of-mouth and the customers come tumbling along after me. I get a fresh injection of ideas when I have new people interested. Even young Karen with her farm-yard ones, has given me a new lease on life."

CHAPTER TWENTY THREE

A Black Experience

Herman Gordon seemed to have gone into hiding so far as the two young boys were concerned. They had heard very little of him other than those answers they got from Jane de Lune, when she popped in or was on the telephone organizing the Art Show at their local school; which was imminent. Herman was the typical expectant father, doting upon his wife and preparing those urgent necessities, such as a room for the babies and the whims and fancies of his Moira. That she demanded a little more of his time than was usual, caused the man to temporarily forget his little fisher friends. One day, the boys threw caution to the winds and asked if they could ring him. It was left to Jeremy to make the call. As Gerard noted.

"I think he likes you better than me!"

"What a lot of rot!" Jeremy expostulated. "Never mind, I will ring him."

Jeremy's mother warned him not to push too hard. If Mister Gordon was unable to take them that was just bad luck and Jeremy would just have to accept the fact. "They are expecting a family, you know!" His mother reminded. Both of the boys' fathers were away at a Farming Convention and were expected to be gone all week-end.

The boys would just have to fish at their usual spot if Herman was too busy.

"Yes Dear?" Moira asked when Jeremy identified himself as the caller.

"How are you feeling Missus Gordon, is the baby here yet?" He awkwardly asked.

"No Jeremy, not yet Dear; in about two months!"

"Gosh. It takes a long time!"

"Yes Dear but we can't rush things, the longer it takes the more healthy the baby will be – what can I do for you?"

"Well, I have not heard from Mister Gordon for yonks and Gerard and I thought he might have forgotten us – now that he is going to be a dad!"

"Oh dear me, no! I shall get him to come and have a chat to you, shall I?"

"Yes'm – please."

"Hello there young Jeremy!" Herman's deep voice sounded. "Have I been neglecting you, Pal?"

"Well, we know you are busy being a dad and all, but we want to know if you can spare some time to take Gerard and me to your special fishing spot. You know the one my dad made the bridge at? We promise to be good but if it is too much trouble, mum said I am not to annoy you. Please Mister Gordon – you can keep all the fish we catch to put in your 'fridge!"

Herman was quiet for a moment, then whispered.

"Just hang on for a second or two Pal, I shall ask my wife if she will let me take you!"

Jeremy heard the receiver being placed upon the telephone table, then the heavy footsteps receding. As from afar, the boy could hear the two adults conversing but he was unable to understand what they were saying. The boy strained his hearing and was rewarded with the sound of Herman approaching the telephone again. It rattled as the man picked up the receiver.

"Hello Jeremy, are you still there?" He asked.

"Yes Sir, Mister Gordon."

"How does this Saturday sound to you?"

"Ripper – gee thank you Mister Gordon!"

"My wife has allowed me to take you just for the morning; she can spare me that long. My sister is coming to stay with her, so that I can get away. I have not been fishing since that last time we all went together. See you about eight o'clock on Saturday morning!"

"Yes Mister Gordon, thank you Sir!"

Eight fifteen had the three fishermen leave Herman's four wheel drive outside the shack.

"Just wait here for a minute or two boys, while I have a look at the explosives shed – won't be long!" Herman hurried away.

"Gosh, we should get some beaut fish today!" Gerard eagerly exclaimed.

"I reckon. It is an ideal day for trout, just a bit cloudy and a slight breeze to ripple the water. Bet I catch the biggest!"

Herman returned, a very worried frown dimmed his features.

"Is something wrong Mister Gordon?" Jeremy tentatively asked.

"Nothing for you boys to be bothered about, someone has broken in to the shed again, but I think they only stole those line-nets that I confiscated. The explosives seem to be intact! I shall catch up with whoever took them. Let us get stuck into catching some good-sized fish!"

All made their ways to the log bridge, to consummate their ultimate passions. A very happy morning elapsed with all three having some luck with their fishing. Herman ruffled the hair upon each boy's head as he bid adieu at the Purcell Farm. "See you another time boys, I must get back to look after my missus."

"Goodbye Mister Gordon and thank you!" Gerard called as the vehicle departed. Herman waved as Jeremy echoed his cobber's farewell.

"What will we do this arvo?" Gerard moaned.

"Dunno – hey – why don't we go riding? Bet Bessie would love a run and I reckon Rosie could be looking for a gallop too!"

Jeremy's keen face brought an answer in the affirmative from his blonde mate.

"Yeah! What say we ride up to the Northern Hill and see can we find those chicken-stealing foxes?"

"Yeah. Should we take Bluey and Sam?" Jeremy suggested. Gerard raised his shoulders.

"Think your dad will let you? I know old Rover is too doddery to keep up with us, but your dogs could run a fox down, I reckon. Let's ask your parents!"

After a quite filling lunch and with the portable telephone down his shirt front, Jeremy led his mate and the two dogs on the journey to the outer paddocks; where the North Hill was located. Most of the time it was the dogs leading, and Jeremy strove hard to have the dogs, trained to his father's whistle, obey him and come to heel. By the time the hills were reached, the dogs had run their initial exuberance out and had come to heel somewhat.

"I reckon we will find foxes close along the boundary fence where the scrubby bushes are!" Jeremy asserted.

"Yes, but foxes like the old blackberry brambles best, 'specially if there are lots of stinging nettles about. My dad reckons the foxes get where it is hard for people to get at them!" Gerard informed.

Sam and Bluey had a field day routing rabbits and the odd quail. Their boundless energy and keen senses kept the two dogs baying and chasing endlessly.

"P'raps we should have told the dogs we are after foxes!" Gerard joked.

Jeremy took the suggestion more seriously.

"Yeah! Wish I grabbed that fox skin out of the hay loft; we could have rubbed it on their noses. Then the dogs would have known what we were after!"

"Let us canter around the boundary fence until we get to that gully. I bet the dogs will put up a fox in there!" Gerard heeled Rosie forwards, Jeremy followed.

The gully was indeed very dense and ideal for a wily old fox's habitat.

Bluey put up a fox almost as soon as he nosed into the scrub, Sam joined the chase and the boys galloped off in gleeful pursuit. For a good kilometre the chase ensued, until finally the fox baffled the dogs by disappearing entirely. Sam and Bluey yelped about in a bewildered frenzy.

"It got away." Gerard called, disgruntled.

"Not to worry, at least we had a good chase – gosh it was fun – let us go and see what that dark blob is, over there amongst the bushes!" Jeremy puzzled.

The boys went ahead, even though the two dogs were still sniffing about where they lost the fox. As the boys neared the thicket where Jeremy fancied he could see a bark humpy, the truth dawned. It was a bark lean-to such as he had read about in one of the library books at school. It appeared to have only recently been vacated, as a couple of potato sacks were on the floor and oddments of civilisation could be seen lying about. There was no sign of anybody who could have been using the shelter though. The two kelpies, Bluey and Sam, came trotting up to the horses; then suddenly they were off, growling as they shot into the bushes beyond the humpy. A frightened childish wail was heard. The boys dismounted. Tying his mount to a bush, Jeremy called the dogs; they remained where they were, growling.

It was a singular sight that the two lads came across. Trembling up in the top of a small bush, with Bluey and Sam standing guard, was a little aborigine boy of about six years of age. He wore only a cotton shirt and a pair of khaki shorts. The boy was bare-footed and his large black eyes protruded in fear.

"Sam, Bluey, heel!" Jeremy ordered.

The dogs came, still eying the little boy. Jeremy patted both dogs.

"Good boy!" He told each of them. "Sit!"

The dogs sat. Jeremy called to the little boy.

"You can come down, the dogs won't hurt you!"

He reached up for the little aborigine boy. The boy clung tighter to the bush, shaking his head.

"It is all right, we won't hurt you!" Gerard smiled. Still the boy shook his head.

"I know, just wait a second Gerard." Jeremy went to his mare.

He removed the sandwiches that he had to take with him, from the saddle-bag. Jeremy offered them to the little boy. He eyed them avidly. Jeremy took a small bite from one sandwich, then again offered them to the child. He slowly reached out a hand, then grabbed the food and began wolfing into the sandwiches. Gerard too, went to his mare. He offered a plastic container of orange juice to the boy, that his mother had equipped him with. The boy took that too, although without snatching. The two older boys waited until the child had finished, then beckoned him down. Slowly he came. Jeremy walked back to the humpy with Gerard, and both sat on the ground outside the lean-to, each held a dog by the collar. The little boy shyly came and he too, sat down but just inside his home.

"What is your name?" Jeremy asked.

The aborigine just looked at his feet. Gerard pointed to himself and said.

"Gerard." Then pointed to his pal and said. "Jeremy."

A small light brightened in the tiny face of the aboriginal child. He pointed to himself.

"Ngalla!"

It became evident that Ngalla had very little knowledge of the English language. The two white boys could not find out what this little aboriginal boy was doing, being left apparently, un-attended. Jeremy extracted the telephone from his shirt, with the intention of ringing his mother to find out what he should do about Ngalla; when suddenly, a very large black man appeared, as though from nowhere. He even took the two dogs by surprise as they wrenched themselves clear of the tight hold the two boys had on them. The aboriginal man stood with a long spear pointed at the two dogs, the while he jabbered in his native dialect, with his son. Ngalla patted his stomach and brandished the empty juice bottle as he answered his father's questions. A very big, toothy smile from the man set the boys at ease. Jeremy called the dogs to heel. They came but still a growl or two rumbled in their throats.

"Ngalla say you good boys. Give food and drink to Ngalla; Djinagalla thank you!" He said.

It was then that the boys noticed a pair of rabbits hanging from Djinagalla's waist band. We make rabbit to eat – boys want some?"

The man's large toothy face beamed as of a crescent moon when he offered a share of his hunt.

"No thank you!" Both boys refused. "Do you and Ngalla live here?" Jeremy queried.

"Little bit, not long, go soon!"

"May I see your boomerang please?" Gerard asked, his eyes hardly taken away from the man's weapons.

"Boy look – not take!" Djinagalla said, as he offered the boomerang which had been hanging from his waist-band; to Gerard. "Goodfellah that one, best Djinagalla make!"

"Gosh, I wish I had a beaut boomerang like that – isn't it great Jeremy?"

He shared a look at the weapon with his cobber. Djinagalla went into the humpy and foraged under one of the potato sacks. He returned with two boomerangs. Both were made of hardwood elbows from branches and were lightly carved. Each had a small imperfection. The one offered to Jeremy had the tip of one wing chipped and the one offered to Gerard, had a slight split to one end.

"No good this one. Whistle in air." Djinagalla informed the speechless lad. "Be good boys and tell no one Djinagalla and Ngalla stay here. We go soon. Good boys, yes?"

"No, we won't tell anyone; gee, thanks!" Gerard agreed.

Both boys mounted, stuffing the heavy boomerangs down their shirt-fronts. Jeremy called the dogs and the visitors departed.

"Bye Ngalla." The boys shouted together.

Ngalla and Djinagalla waved back. The boys rode away towards home.

The two kelpies had been having the time of their lives and were just about run out. Their tongues hung low as the two dogs trotted beside the two walking mares. The dogs panted heavily.

"The dogs need a drink Gerard, and a rest. I think we should head for the north dam so they can rest up, they have been running hard. Dad will kill me if I run too much condition off them!"

"Okay!" Gerard agreed.

The boys cantered their mounts gently to the said destination. The north dam was rarely visited by humans. It was mainly the animal life which abounded in this wilder section of the Purcell Farm that used the water from this dam. Matt had a hundred head of his older sheep using this far paddock, just to keep the grass down. Occasionally one would fall to foxes but as there was an abundance of rabbits on and about the lower slopes of the North Hill, the sheep were relatively safe from this threat. Both kelpies knew of the dam from their occasional forays in to this paddock, when the sheep had to be mustered, so they headed straight for the welcome drink that they both needed. As there was nowhere to tie the ponies, both boys 'ground hitched' their steeds just away from the dam; after the ponies had watered. The boys wandered through the surrounding rushes to the water's edge as the ponies nibbled the lush grass.

"Gee! I reckon we should bring your big yabby net here Jeremy. There would be heaps of yabbies in this dam!" Gerard stated, emphatically.

"It is a long way to carry the net on bicycles though!" Jeremy defended.

"We could ride the ponies again. It would not be so bad on the ponies."

"Yeah, I s'pose!" Jeremy admitted.

A low snarling growl emanated from the throat of Sam, one of the kelpies. The other, Bluey, joined in. Their eyes were focussed on the ground. Upon looking to find the cause of the kelpies' dissent, Jeremy cautioned.

"Snake! Gerard be careful, the dogs have found a snake!"

"Crikey! There is one here too – gee – the place is crawling with them. Let's get out of here!" Gerard called.

"Take your time and look where you are treading!" Jeremy advised.

Both boys safely made their ways clear of the dangerous area and headed once again, for home. Once home, Jeremy proudly showed off his newly acquired boomerang to his parents and Karen. His father had returned from his meeting. "My word Son that is a real boomerang, not one of those shop-made toys. Where on earth did you find that?" His father asked.

"Oops! I promised I wouldn't tell, Dad!"

"Oh I see. I know you did not steal it, because I trust you and if you have promised someone not to tell, then you have met a stranger. Could you tell me why a stranger would give you a valuable, real boomerang Son?"

The boy struggled with his conscience momentarily, and then drawled.

"We found his little son up on the North Hill and we fed him my sandwiches. He gave Gerard and me a boomerang each and asked us not to tell where they were!"

"Thank you Son, I won't ask you to break your promise and you may keep the boomerang!"

"Yes Daddy!"

Matt and Yvonne discussed the matter when the children were gone.

"I worry about Jeremy wandering all over the place and meeting with these strangers!" Yvonne declared.

"This one is all right Dear, he is known to me."

"Oh?"

"It will be Djinagalla and his son Ngalla; they often camp on our property up there on their way to town to sell artefacts. He has been doing the same for years. He would know of our son, Djinagalla worked for me once!"

CHAPTER TWENTY FOUR

The Art Exhibition

Came the day of the Parents and Teachers Meeting and Yvonne, true to her word, had organized with the chairperson and other committee members, for her and Jane to display and sell their Bark Pictures at the local venue on the day of the meeting. A proviso was that the artists should donate a percentage of their sales to the school coffers. Yvonne offered ten percent as a teaser. It was graciously accepted as Yvonne knew it would be; the school committee ever seeking donations to help with its upkeep. Jane was suitably impressed with these arrangements. The gathering numbered thirty souls including the teachers and Jane, as the guest speaker. Her subject of course, was her hobby; Bark Pictures. After a short official welcome by the school Principal, the business of the meeting got under way and that was speedily despatched. As guest speaker, Jane was then introduced and gave a notable speech. Her question time produced a host of inquiries from very interested parents. When she was asked if the Bark Picture hobby was suitable for children to learn, Jane immediately pointed out the five exhibits that Karen Purcell had entered, impressing upon the parents that in her only officially entered exhibit; Karen won a Special Award in the Novice Section. Consequently the little girl's entire five pictures on display were sold out. Although Karen's pictures were only priced at ten dollars each, that was forty five dollars into her bank account, which would enable backing boards and frames to be bought; so that she could continue with her hobby and not have her parents out of pocket on her behalf. The little girl would be self-sufficient with her expenses. The five dollars her pictures earned for the school funds, was duly noted and included in a letter of thanks posted to her parents. Yvonne was overwhelmed by the interest shown in their exhibition. Many of the other mothers mobbed her and Jane, in an endeavour to learn more about this unusual hobby. Jeremy's teacher, Miss Purdie, sought Yvonne and gushed over her pictures and those of her daughter.

"How clever of you to teach Karen the art of making those wonderful pictures, I bought one of Karen's pictures; it is the one of a paddock full of sheep. Mind you, they do not look at all like sheep close up, but when one stands back – oh my – it is a wonderful farm scene!"

"Thank you Jean, but I did not teach Karen – it was Jane de Lune – she is also my tutor. I am so thrilled with this new hobby and I am going to push the school board, to include the art as one of the Art Class activities. I believe it would be a marvellous pastime for the whole school!" Yvonne thrilled.

"Pity the local trees then." Jean smiled, impishly.

"It is possible to overcome that by banning the children from skinning the township trees. If a couple of the interested parents went out of a week-end, then they could gather enough pieces to supply the whole school for months. That would be the best way to address the problem." Yvonne suggested.

Jean Purdie agreed, and then asked. "How did you find this wonderful Jane de Lune? Her pictures are so varied and intriguing. Do her services come at a great expense?"

"No, on the contrary, Jane has become a very dear friend. I met her through young Jeremy's association with her brother, you remember Herman Gordon, the Game Warden?"

"Oh yes, is Jane his sister? Well I never!" Jean was silent for a moment, thinking. Then she confided. "You know Yvonne, that young man of yours has marked improvement with his schooling, since the advent of Herman Gordon's influence upon him. The boy is so good in class this year and so obedient and polite, I sometimes wonder if it is the same boy we had last year. His class-mate Gerard has also improved. That man has had a great part in that, I feel sure!"

Jane came bubbling over.

"Yvonne! Excuse me, but I just sold another two of my pictures. That one you thought was my best – the spring scene – and the snow-capped mountain!"

"Oh Jane, you must be thrilled that we are doing so well! I would like you to meet Jean Purdie – Jeremy's teacher – Jane de Lune." Yvonne introduced the two.

Jean congratulated Jane on her talk and the exhibition.

"Yvonne tells me you are Herman Gordon's sister, Jane! I was just saying to her how well the boys he has influenced have been doing with their schooling!"

"How sweet of you to say that, I shall certainly pass it on to Herman, he will be so pleased. He is to be a father himself in a couple of months and it will do him and Moira the world of good; to know that he is a good tutor!" The School Principal interrupted.

"Pardon me ladies but Missus de Lune is in demand elsewhere. Would you excuse us please? This way, I have a very important man who wishes to speak with you!" He ushered Jane away.

The Principal hurried Jane over to a quite imposing man. He was the centre of attention amongst a group of six, three of the local traders and their wives. He had the mien of a man of authority and his attire was that of a person who took great pride in his personal appearance. He excused himself graciously from the group with whom he was conversing, when he caught the eye of the Principal, who was accompanying the guest speaker in his direction.

"Ah James, so this is the artist whose work I so admire!"

The Principal introduced Jane to Mister Geoffrey Rogerson, Director of the Art Gallery.

"So pleased to meet you, Mister Rogerson!" Jane acknowledged.

Her spirits soared when the magic words 'Director of the local Art Gallery', were sounded.

"If I may call you Jane, please call me Geoffrey!" He smiled as he extended his hand.

Jane was flattered by the extreme interest that Geoffrey showed in the whole of the Bark Picture Exhibition. His keen eye to detail had her enthralled as he delved deeply into the meanings of the shading barks and creativeness of colour arrangements. Geoffrey bemoaned the fact that whilst concentrating on the adult offering, he had neglected to purchase one of the ones made by 'the young lady', as he referred to Karen. Jane interrupted his colourful harangue into the young lady's Art Works.

"I shall introduce you to the girl's mother and perchance you would admire to select from those that Karen has at home?"

"Really? But of course, the mother of the little girl would be here. How thoughtful of you! Could we meet her now, please?" He asked.

Yvonne too, was flattered that an Art Director would be so interested in their exhibition and more so, that he wished to acquire one of her daughter's works.

"Would next Saturday evening be a suitable time for me to visit you, Yvonne; say at around eight thirty?" That settled, Geoffrey became embroiled with other people as the Principal once again, whisked him away to meet yet another interested parent. His services seemed to be in high demand as would-be purchasers of these unusual pictures, sought professional advice.

Jane and Yvonne went to the buffet table for refreshments and to exchange notes on the progress and success of their daring venture in infiltrating a Parents and Teachers gathering.

"I am absolutely flabbergasted that people would be so interested in my hobby pictures Jane!" Yvonne excitedly confided to her tutor. "Do you know I have sold seven already and there are four more set aside for the Prentiss people to make up their minds about. I am positive they will take three, but the fourth one, he does not like. Perhaps he will settle on some other one."

"That is why I have my business cards made up. People can ring me later, after they have had time to consider. Sometimes, when people get back home and try to decide where to hang their bark pictures, they come to the conclusion that the place they envisaged, is not suitable after all. It is then that I get a 'phone call asking for another picture, so they can balance the décor. With a bark picture at either side of a central motif perhaps, or even where one does not appear to fill the space properly. You really should arrange to have your own personal business cards, Yvonne. It will pay you to do so!"

"Yes, I dare say!" Yvonne agreed, and then asked. "How are you selling Jane? You seem to have been selling heaps. I have seen so many sold stickers on your offerings; have you any unsold?"

"Oh my word yes! One always takes home seventy five percent of the art works brought along to these hangings. I know of fifteen that are definite sales and there are another couple of maybes, but we have all done exceptionally well, considering that this was an impromptu hanging. We should be well satisfied with our efforts!" Jane enthused.

"What about young Karen? Her first public hanging for sale and she ends up with a whopping one hundred percent sell-out, the cheeky little imp!" Yvonne proudly exclaimed.

Geoffrey Rogerson interrupted the two ladies. He had come up unnoticed by them.

"Oh Jane – Yvonne, could I have your time for a few minutes, please? I have something to discuss with you both!"

"Why, of course!" The two spoke in unison.

Geoffrey led them around their exhibition, prattling on about the merits of this exhibit or the downside of that; occasionally stopping to announce.

"I have selected this one and that one for inclusion in my gallery!"

In all, the Art Director selected six works; four of Jane's and two of Yvonne's.

"As these six will be on show in our new 'Nature Chamber', I shall expect a fairly decent reduction collectively; could you arrange that?"

Both artists readily agreed, in deference to the expected visit to Yvonne's home on the coming Saturday evening.

On the way home from the Parents and Teachers meeting, Jane was moved to comment.

"Gosh Yvonne, I am so glad we met. I have sold very well and unexpectedly so, at this Parents and Teachers meeting. I must try other schools, as I really think we are on to something in that area. I am so glad that Herman met your youngster!"

"You are glad?" Yvonne scoffed. "What about Matt and me? To say nothing of the good he has done with his influence over Jeremy – and young Gerard. You heard what the teacher Jean said. I fully endorse that too; the boy's behaviour and school work definitely has improved. Herman has been good for all of us!"

"My word, now that I look back over the years, he has been a wonderful brother for me too. You know, I used to bully him when I was a teenager and he was just a little bit of a kid. I remember that although I loved my little brother in his early years, I began to resent him as a mill-stone when mum made me mind him. I wanted to get out and meet with the young men I was infatuated with, yet there I was; stuck at home babysitting my kid brother. Gosh I can remember how I hated him when our parents came home and doted upon him. I felt left out and just used. Now that I look back, I realise that it was all just a part of growing up. Herman grew up so quickly and became so strong in his teens, and for all of the hard time I had given him as a kid, he was so protective of me. You know, when I first told him I was going to get married, he befriended John before John was aware Herman was my brother; to satisfy himself that John was worthy of me!"

The next five days dragged for Yvonne. After the success of her venture into the world of art, and the many congratulatory telephone calls from her peers; Yvonne believed that she had a great future in her newly found hobby. Jane de Lune was invited back for the evening visit by the local Art Gallery Director, Geoffrey Rogerson. It really was a foregone conclusion, as her knowledge and expertise in the area of Bark Picture making, was by far, superior to Yvonne's. Also, it was an opportunity for Jane to select some of her better works from home, to embellish those of Yvonne and Karen. The children were formally introduced to the great man when he duly arrived at the appointed time.

"I am very pleased to meet you", young man!"

Geoffrey acknowledged, as he gently shook hand with Jeremy.

"Yes sir! How do you do?" The boy replied, and then moved into the background to continue with his school project. Karen was aglow with excitement and dressed prettily on this momentous occasion for her. She really had no idea just what an Art Director did, but was suitably impressed by the fact that the man was very important, and that he had come especially to see Karen and perhaps buy a picture which she had made.

"My, my, what a pretty little girl, how are you my dear? So you are the one who makes such wonderful pictures out of bark!"

Karen nodded vigorously, her black curls danced.

"Do you know, I have come just to see some more of your pictures? May I?"

Geoffrey smiled at Karen. She took him by the hand and led him in to her bedroom.

"There are some on the walls, they are my best ones and I have two in Mummy's room. Do you want to see them too?" Karen asked as she turned her wide, enquiring eyes up to the visitor.

"My word I do, but may I study these first?" Geoffrey asked.

"Mmm!" The curly hair danced again.

Geoffrey Rogerson made notes in his notebook as he quietly walked from picture to picture around Karen's bedroom. There were three pictures hanging upon the walls and two on her dressing table. He just patted Karen's head, saying.

"Yes, these are lovely – er – you have two in your mummy's room, you say?"

Geoffrey asked, looking to Yvonne.

"Please Geoffrey, this way. I selected one of them and the other is the first one Karen made back home here. I have a soft spot for both of them!"

Yvonne proudly showed off her daughter's art-work.

"My my, you do have good taste Yvonne. Could I select this one?"

He pointed to the picture that Yvonne had selected.

"Oh dear! I was hoping I may have retained that one!"

"Well of course, if it has all that much sentimental value – but
-" he looked over his spectacles at Yvonne "the gallery will pay forty

five dollars for it; providing we can place a photograph of the artist beside the picture!"

Yvonne was flabbergasted.

"Really?" She turned to Karen. "Karen Dear, Mister Rogerson would like to buy this picture that you gave to Mummy. Do you mind if we sell it to him? He is going to hang it in the Art Gallery with your picture beside it, so everyone will know what nice pictures you make! Is that all right Dear, can he take it?"

"But I made that one just for you Mummy!"

"Yes, and it is lovely, but I think you can make a much better one for Mummy now. Don't you think?" Yvonne kissed her daughter on the forehead.

"Mmm! I know – we can go and get some really new bark!" Karen brightened.

"Yes dear and I will make a nice new one for you too!" Yvonne hugged Karen.

Geoffrey had a field day as he studied his way through both Yvonne's and Jane's gatherings of bark pictures.

"You know Ladies, I have decided, in fact I made up my mind the day after your exhibition at the school, that if you will allow me to select say – thirty or so of your Bark Pictures – on consignment; I will organize a one-weeks showing. I have set aside what I think I explained at the school, and that is, a 'Nature Chamber'. Because these pictures are from natural materials, they are perfect for inclusion in our 'Special Display'! To open this chamber to the public, I see no better introduction than a J. de Lune and Y. Purcell Bark Picture hanging for a whole week. I envisage the run to be from Friday evening until the Sunday of the second week-end. Could I have some sort of response to this suggestion?"

Geoffrey poised himself for the expected reply.

"What are the terms?" Jane studiously asked.

"Just for the hangings there will be no charge. If we decide upon sales only, the gallery will demand twenty five percent of sales. However, if you allow the weeks hanging to be finalised on the Sunday afternoon with an auction, then the cost will only be the usual seventeen percent, plus handling, which will be passed on to the consumer. Think this deal over and let me know of your decision by three-thirty on Wednesday!"

Both Jane and Yvonne discussed their stupendous good fortune and duly rang Geoffrey Rogerson to answer in the affirmative. The auction eventuated to the benefit of all, even young Karen. The art of Bark Picture making became a firmly established pastime all around.

CHAPTER TWENTY FIVE

The Mentor is fulfilled

Life for Herman and Moira Gordon became more leisurely, as each in their own way, prepared for the enormous change in their lifestyles. The lively activity foreign to them, in which the two were embroiled due to them being associated with Jeremy, Gerard and Karen; had not only given the childless couple a glimpse of life with a family of their own, but had been somewhat of a warning to take life easy, whilst they could. Both realised that the coming family would be time-consuming initially and both frustrating and wonderful at the same time; during the next twenty or so years. Although Moira and Herman expected an increased work-load, the wonderful thought of them nurturing and raising a family of their own, had the two awaiting the new arrivals with glowing hearts. The three young children, who had so much of an impact on Moira and Herman, were blissfully unaware of the important part in the lives of their mentor and his wife that they played. That pictures of the three children that were on display in the Gordon home, was evidence of the esteem in which that household held for their lively little guests. Herman still had his work to attend and it would now be doubly necessary to have that stronghold, for more mouths would soon be relying upon this security. As Pat was well recovered from his accident and rehabilitation, he accompanied

Herman on a trip to Fletcher's Falls. The object of their mission, was to give the Council their input into a recommendation put to Council by the Police, for a safety fence to be erected at the site of Pat's accident, to prevent any further similar mishap eventuating. The Game Wardens were not really surprised to find that a vehicle had but only recently used the flat river bank, easily accessible from the road. That the tyre marks did continue into the heavy scrub, gave the men to consider the reason for the vehicle to have forced its way into the denseness of the scrub. There was no real need to take a vehicle in there. A fishing party could easily walk the few hundred metres along the river bank, which extended from the falls. The Game Wardens knew that a large cliff-face halted any further progress by a vehicle, so they decided to investigate. As the vehicle left only one set of tyre tracks, it stood to reason that it had not returned and was still somewhere ahead. When the two men came in sight of the vehicle, Herman was staggered to find that it was the Station Wagon in which the lady and the two teenagers had become bogged, up at Cooper's Creek. Consequently, he jotted down the vehicle description and the registration number, recalling that he had already caught the owner twice and that he was still in custody; or so Herman thought. Forewarned, the two Fishing Inspectors crept stealthily onwards. It was another forty metres along the river bank before the two Game Wardens sighted their quarry. Surprise upon surprise! Not only was the woman who became bogged there but also her husband, the man Herman thought was safely locked away! The miscreants were again netting the river illegally. There was no way out for them, as other than swim the cold waters of the river, the cliff face and the officers themselves were a barrier to the escape of the husband wife team. In disgust at once more being apprehended, the man threw down forcibly, the bag of fish that he had been filling. Two more fish were still flipping upon the bank at his feet. Resignedly, the two people awaited the coming arrests. Herman was so disgusted at the outright defiance of the laws that these people flagrantly abused, that he was moved to comment.

"Will you two ever learn that this type of activity is illegal and spoils the fishing for honest folk?" The two just shrugged. The woman spoke.

"He can't get a job, we have to live somehow!" Herman glared at them.

"From what I see, he doesn't want a job. When I inspect those line-nets, I am fairly sure that they will be the ones I confiscated initially and then put in the explosives shed. You will certainly have added charges of 'breaking and entering', to answer now!"

"Tell you what!" The man said. "If you do not lay charges against us, I promise we will never 'line net' again. I will make a fire right now and burn these nets in front of you – what say – gimme a break, please?"

Herman looked at the man in disgust, and then enlightened him.

"I took two sets of netting off you upon two different occasions. You were charged and jailed the second time, and then this lady and two boys turned up with another set of netting, old though it was. That makes three sets of nets. Burning the one set still leaves two others and who is to say where or when you will get another set?" He paused, considering, then asked. "Anyway, how come you are not in detention? You were charged with stealing as well as line-netting!"

The man smugly retorted.

"Had an appeal, the magistrate saw that we were just innocent bystanders of Terrence Grail's thieving spree, so he reduced our sentence to another fine!"

"You will never learn and breaking into the explosives shed is the one thing that will seal your fate. I shall put forwards a very strong argument for putting you out of temptation's way. This time you will get a custodial sentence. My rivers are for honest folk to fish from and enjoy. I will not have people like you spoiling the fishing for the many!"

Herman and Pat booked the man and wife team; only regretting that his accomplice was not involved this time. He did feel a little sorry for their teenage boy and his friend though. When all of the details of their arrests were finalised and those nets once again confiscated, Herman and Pat began the job which had them come to Fletcher's Falls in the first place. They studied in detail, the area just off the track down to the grassy bank of the river and decided that a safety rail alongside the gravel road would suffice as a protection from a repeat accident. They also recommended that an ingress opening should be provided, leading down from the behind tree that caused Pat's vehicle to bounce off it and enter the river.

A week before Moira Gordon was expected to give birth, the telephone rang. It was a call from the Purcell Family. They wished to pop in for a visit and to present their gift to celebrate the new expected arrivals. Moira was sitting upon the settee, covered by a rug and glowing with good health when the visitors came. Herman welcomed the Purcell Family and had refreshments available.

"My goodness Moira!" Yvonne happily stated. "The house will not be the same again after the new arrivals are here! How are you coping, is Herman looking after you properly?"

"We won't stay long." Matt assured. "We must get the young ones back home and in bed. You will have these problems too!"

All sat about Moira as Herman passed tea, cakes and orange juice around his most welcome guests.

"Can we give them their presents now, Dad?" Jeremy asked.

Karen just stood, holding one of the presents and nodding her head with vigour; eyes sparkling.

"Yes children, do it nicely like we are supposed to do it – be polite!" Matt gave his approval. Jeremy walked over to the Gordon's as Herman sat by his wife, who held his hand. They waited expectantly.

"Mister and Missus Gordon, Dad, Mum, Karen and me, want you to have these nice gifts for the new babies. We had to give them to you early so you could take pictures – oops – now I have spoiled the surprise!"

Jeremy looked impishly at his parents as he offered Herman the camera. Karen passed the photograph album to Moira and gave her a sloppy kiss upon the cheek.

"They are from us!" She triumphantly claimed.

"Oh! Thank you dear. May I open them now, or should I wait for the family to arrive?"

"No. You have to open them now!" Karen demanded. "I want to see them too!"

Then Yvonne encouraged.

"I am sure Herman will want to get used to using the camera so that he can take perfect pictures when the time comes. The birth will only happen once with each child you know; you may have three or four and it is always best to get in early with your photographs of the babies!"

"Yes! We missed out in the first few weeks with Jeremy, made up for that with Karen though!" Matt grinned.

Karen also gave Herman a big kiss. He gave her a cuddle. Jeremy, not to be left out, went to Moira.

"I hope you like the presents for the family!" He appeared a little awkward.

Moira beckoned the boy a little closer to her.

"I love them Jeremy, what a very thoughtful present to give us. May I kiss you dear?" "Mmm!" Jeremy reddened slightly.

Herman called the boy to him.

"Come here little fishing Pal, I have something I want to give to you!"

Jeremy came, expectantly.

"This!" Herman squeezed the boy to him. "You are not too big that I can't give you a cuddle. I need to thank you and Karen and Gerard, because by having you go fishing and camping. In fact by just being about us, we decided to have our own family!"

Jeremy looked up at his mentor in surprise.

"Yes Pal, you three made us yearn to have our own family and we want to thank you. Here, I would like you and Karen to have these and I have another for Gerard too!"

Herman gave each of the children an envelope.

"Wait until you get back home before you open them; will you?"

"Yes Mister Gordon. Thank you!"

The Purcell Family left, leaving the Gordon's a little melancholy.

Upon arriving home, Jeremy and Karen quickly opened the presents that the Gordon's gave them.

"Wow!" Jeremy gasped in awe. "Have a look Dad. It is a wrist watch – it's a ripper too!"

"Really. May I see it Son?" His father asked.

"I have one too – Mummy – look!"

Karen eagerly ran to her parents to show off her surprise present.

"The cunning devil!" Yvonne shook her head, disbelievingly. "Herman had them already arranged before we rang to take the camera and photo album. He seems to forever be one jump ahead of everybody!"

It was Matt's turn to be nonplussed.

"Look here!" He said as he studied the inscription upon the watch that he was holding. "It reads: - 'To Jeremy, our Pal. M. and H. Gordon.'!"

"What does mine say Mummy?" Karen was agog with curiosity.

"I shall put my glasses on Dear. Ah, there! It reads: - 'To Karen, all our love. M. and H. Gordon.'!"

Karen clapped her hands.

"Can I put it on now, please Mummy?"

Both children beamed happily at their newly acquired time-pieces.

"Right. Off to bed children – clean your teeth!" Matt ordered.

It was just before they were due to retire for the night that Moira felt her pains at an increased rate.

"Herman!" She called. "I think it is time – grab the bags!"

"Are you sure, My Sweet? We do not want to look foolish!" He was at her side in an instant.

"Yes Love, I am sure. Please let us hurry!"

Herman gently assisted Moira to her feet, grabbed the bags which were ever ready and at hand; then made his very pregnant wife comfortable in the rear seat of her sedan. He rang their doctor to make the necessary arrangements, and then they hurried to the hospital.

The birth was not complicated and the healthy twins made their entry into the world, with very lusty cries for attention.

"They take after their father in that department!" Moira happily breathed, with a sigh of relief.

"Bouncing baby boy and a bonnie little lady!" The midwife cheerily announced.

"Oh Herman!" Moira gasped, as she received a loving kiss from her very proud husband, the new father. "Our most fervent prayers have been answered – one of each – oh Darling, I am so thrilled.

The babies were cleaned, wrapped and passed to their glowing mother. Herman had a bright-eyed grin upon his features, which threatened to split his ears. "Mother, you look so gorgeous and comfortable there with our two most beautiful babies, that I -!"

Moira cut in impishly.

"Fiddlesticks! I know they look like a pair of prunes Dear, but just you wait a day or two and then you will know what beautiful is – oh Herman - I can see that our two angels will turn out to be the most wonderful children!"

Herman kissed his wife and gently touched his lips to each of his new-born children's heads.

"Sorry Dears!" A nurse said, as she and her assistant came to take the little ones away. "We have to relieve you of these little tricks. Tidy up, weighing and measuring, health checks; all that sort of thing. They will be back soon. You two have a last cuddle, and then you may leave us for a bit, Father!"

"Yes Maám!" Herman brightly answered, before that cuddle and then returning to wait with the other fathers and expectant fathers. When he entered the waiting room; Jane rushed up to him.

"Hermie! Are they here yet, how is Moira, are they healthy – can we see them – are they -??"

"Steady on Sis!" Herman hugged his sister. "One of each, both healthy; Moira's fine!"

"Congratulations to you both. Oh isn't this great? I can't wait to see them!"

Jane kissed her brother on the cheek, affectionately.

After two days at the hospital, Moira was ready to go home and take her family with her; however the doctors advised that another day of rest would be advisable. After all, once home and on her own, except for post-natal visits by the mid-wife; her life would become quite hectic. Assuring the doctor that her sister-in-law would be on hand and at her service for awhile; the medical man was content to allow Moira to quit the hospital, on the fourth day after the births. Jane seemed to have a new lease on life, once the twins were at home with their parents. Naming the children was not really a problem with the Gordon's. They had settled that problem months beforehand. When twins were surely predicted, Jeremy and Gerard immediately popped in to Herman's mind. If a girl or girls were to be born, then Jane and Karen became bandied about. Nothing definite was settled upon until the parents were definitely assured of the sexes of their coming babies. When it was a fact that the couple were to have one of each, the choices became obvious. Moira was most adamant that Herman's sister should be honoured, by christening the baby girl after her. Herman then strongly endorsed that wish. The boy gave them food for thought however. If they selected one of the young lads over the other in preference of name, they felt that the boy child would be only half named. Jeremy Gerald Gordon did not seem to gel, nor did Gerard Jeremy Gordon. Moira solved that problem too, when she suggested that Herman's close friend and work-mate Patrick should have the honour. The boy child would be christened, Patrick Herman Gordon, allowing the boy to also carry his father's given name.

Six weeks after the birth of their twins, Herman and Moira invited all of their friends to the christening. Jane and Patrick were asked to be God-parents, an honour both instantly jumped at. The Purcell's and the Lonards were also invited to attend the ceremony. As the service was to be held mid-week, the children of both families were still at school and therefore, were not present. The christening went without blemish or incident, so Patrick Herman Gordon and Jane Moira Gordon, were christened with the blessings of the church. The very happy couple were inundated with gifts from well-wishers. Jane spent most of the day taking snapshots, not only with her camera but with the new one belonging to her brother and sister-in-law. Matt and Percy quietly took Herman aside to congratulate him and his wife on the occasion of the christening of their children. Both warmly shook Herman by the hand.

Matt spoke for him and Percy and their wives.

"We all wish you and Moira well on your newest venture into parenthood, but Herman; we have a special 'thank you' to you in another category. You have been a great 'Mentor' to our children and we warmly thank you. Your children will have the same benefit of a constant guiding light throughout their lives. You have no idea how much your input into our children's lives has helped them, and us; from the bottom of our hearts – thank you Herman – and Moira!"

THE END